The
Tomb
Opens

Amel Abouelhassan

iUniverse, Inc.
Bloomington

THE TOMB OPENS

iUniverse books may be ordered through booksellers or by contacting:

iUniverse
1663 Liberty Drive
Bloomington, IN 47403
www.iuniverse.com
1-800-Authors (1-800-288-4677)

ISBN: 978-1-4759-5391-6 (sc)
ISBN: 978-1-4759-5392-3 (ebk)

Printed in the United States of America

iUniverse rev. date: 10/29/2012

Table of Contents

Acknowledgements

No one walks entirely alone on the journey of life. People we meet everyday have an impact on us, when we allow them to. I am no different, and if I am to thank those who believed enough in me to encourage me to put this work into publication, I'd like to start with my own family, I'd like to thank:

My mother Thanaa, for helping me along the way and continuously encouraging me to value my thoughts, to verbalize my ideas, and to share my insights with the world as I always wished.

My husband Hazem, for being there for me – supporting my passion to express my feelings, and to live my dreams in writing; and for tolerating the long hours I spent in putting my novel together.

My brother Mohamed, for his continuous presence through the ups and downs of writing my novel; and always advising me to take it easy on myself whenever he sensed that my enthusiasm was wearing me out.

My sister Yasmin, for relentlessly walking beside me, sharing my dream of bringing this story to the light, and being the wonderful person that she is.

My kids: Sherief and Lydia, for reading parts of my novel, motivating me to write more, and for their endless love.

Also, I'd like to thank all my friends, who demonstrated eagerness to listen and acknowledge the urge I had, to write this novel and the message I wanted to deliver.

And last but never the least, I'd like to thank my readers who'll take the time to join me on this heartfelt story and live with me its incidents and events. I hope you love it.

Thanks,
Amel Abouelhassan

Disclaimer

Much of this story is based on facts. However this is a work of fiction. Names, characters, places and incidents either are products of the author's imagination or are used fictitiously. Any resemblance to actual events or locales or persons, living or dead, is entirely coincidental.

The Tomb Opens

CHAPTER ONE

Deadly Mission

Buttons are clipped, black hat is brushed, suit is ironed, tie, white shirt, and last but never the least, clean white gloves stretch and bend to embrace my hands. I put on my polished shoes and I am on my way to my morning client Mr. Saqr, the immigration officer assistant, of the Canadian Embassy in Cairo.

"Good morning, Saad," all my early-riser neighbors greet me as I smile, nod my head and drive my relatively big cab through the narrow and bumpy road.

I drop Mr. Saqr off at the embassy. "I need to leave in an hour; will you wait for me, Saad please?"

"Sure," I grab a magazine, stick my nose in the pages and wait for the 60 minutes to elapse. I am already prepared to hear "Oh my god, my dream came true", as Mr. Saqr conveys the happy news of the visa being approved and issued. People tend to be so dramatic that I feel as if I am on Oprah.

But to my surprise, come the first Monday of June 2010; things change immensely. Maybe it's due to the world's economy crisis that the dream train runs out of fuel, and gets replaced by an ancient multi-stop steam train.

Instead of the happy tears, I see frozen looks on four faces shocked and taken aback upon hearing Mr. Saqr's news:
"Canada always opens its doors for immigrants. Canada believes that it's with the power of diversity that its economy, industry and balanced culture will keep to flourish. HOWEVER, recently some immigrants would return to their homeland, make some trouble, ask Canada to pull them back and

when the international relations can't facilitate that in a timely manner, those immigrants sue the Canadian government.

This causes Canada and the taxpayers a lot of money. Canada's welcoming policy remains the same, but the profile of eligible candidates has been updated. Canada needs productive personnel, people who are ready to work; people who are willing to share their experience, educate others and be civilized role models.

There is a workshop that each one of you needs to go through and whoever finishes their part successfully, will qualify to be a Canadian immigrant."

This is super interesting. I throw the boring magazine and listen intently. The workshop dictates that the four candidates immigrate locally to Aswan for three months.

"Nadeem – you're assigned the mission of 'raising the awareness against authoritative corruption'.
Salma – you're assigned the mission of 'developing the sense of belonging, pride and integrity'.
Ziko – you're assigned the mission of 'cultivating civilized and productive attitude'.
Dr. Rashad – you're assigned the mission of 'improving the tolerance and opening the heart and mind to accept others'.
Your target is the Egyptians in Aswan, locals or otherwise," Mr. Saqr finishes what I find as very amusing.

"What does this mean?"
"I don't get it"
"What's your point?"
"What does Aswan have anything to do with this?"
"This sounds like hieroglyphs!" they snap one after the other like a row of domino tiles falling.

Mr. Saqr's jokes casually: "It's true; only – you're still Egyptians and you should understand hieroglyphs." They don't laugh. They stare. Mr. Saqr clears his voice:

"To facilitate such mission, we can arrange for a cab chauffeur to be with you at all times. We'll make reservations for you in one of the hotels at the heart area of Aswan. You'll pack, leave and lose touch with friends and family for quite some time. I'll provide you with a plan and you'll hand-in your program and status reports to me; something measurable and visual that can help in my assessment. You can take some time to think about it."

Four iced-lemonades are offered to sooth the rising distress, as the four individuals try to contemplate what they just heard.

Mr. Saqr leans towards me slightly and puts on his quieter tone: "Saad, we've been working together for years and I have always admired your courteous attitude. I'd like to offer you this contract as the primary chauffeur. It is a long-term commitment but I can't think of someone else to trust. If you agree, you'll find the monetary reward pretty satisfying. Think about it and let me by tomorrow, will you?"

Four tall glasses get laid on the table, all licked empty. Nadeem, Ziko, Dr. Rashad and Salma accept what destiny has crafted for them. They decide to go on their survivors' mission uncertain what to do or how to do it. Mr. Saqr looks at me. "Sure, why not?" I agree too.

Cairo wakes up on a sunny morning and I just can't help but wonder why anyone would choose the snow over the sun. As always my mother's voice pops into my head - happens all the time when work-related doubts and concerns knock at the door of my brain. Without permission, also as always, she'd lovingly say, *'you think you know better, ha? Just get busy* 'حبيبي – habiby' (my love), and do your job,' – I miss her though.

I stop the cab and before ringing his cell, sturdy almost senior Dr. Rashad emerges from the four-storey brick building. "Good, you're on time. You want to be respected; you have to be on time."

If I'm not mistaken, this is praise, yet somehow the mechanism that handles Dr. Rashad's thick eyebrows seems to have only one setting: frowning. The frown is harmonized by quite disgusted pair of lips, which although freakishly thin, yet shows clearly under the shadow of his umbrella-like moustache.

On our way to pick up the second passenger, Dr. Rashad complains about the bumpy roads, the voice of the old man calling out for the honey he is selling, the quality of the merchandize nowadays and the way it is arranged in store windows, the persistence of the gas station worker to sell us anything, be it a tissue box or a dashboard cleaner or wipers.

Ziko is a lot lighter in mood than Dr. Rashad, which is such a hilarious irony, since Dr. Rashad is skinny and Ziko is round in shape from head to toe. "Come on buddy, we're fortunate the sky didn't fall on our heads just yet, despite all the pollution."

"I'd appreciate it, if you'd address me as Doctor when you talk to me."

"Sure. Hey, Saad, play us some music, will you."
I put on the songs channel. Dr. Rashad sighs.

"I know … isn't the music these days terrible? I agree with you on that, Dr. Buddy," mocks Ziko.

I have Grumpy and Funny and now I'm about to pick up 'Your Highness', a mid-thirties guy. You see him, the way he walks, talks, dresses; even his sunglasses that look especially peculiar and you have to address him 'Sir'.

"Who is the little buddy?" asks Ziko pointing at the two-year old boy accompanying Sir Nadeem.

"My son, Bassim."

"Hello, there, buddy," says Ziko enthusiastically. "Sorry about his mom."
Sir Nadeem nods silently.

"What? What happened to the boy's mother?" in a hushed tone Dr. Rashad asks curiously.

"I don't know, but she wasn't at the embassy before and she isn't here now, so he is either widowed or divorced, which in both cases isn't good news for the little fellow."

Dr. Rashad looks at Ziko for a while in a mix of disbelief and dismay. Even though he can't help switching his eyebrows to a different setting, the muscles on his face compliment his feelings: his lips close and flatten into an even thinner line with corners bending towards his chin; his nostrils open widely and exhale generously and two more creases squeeze themselves on his already busy forehead.

The only entertainer we are lucky to have is Ziko until I make the last stop to pick up the 'beauty'. An old lady accompanies her.

"This is it, Salma? You are leaving your nana just like that?"

"As soon as I settle, nana, I'm bringing you over."

"I'm like the fish sweetheart, and Egypt is my water, I leave it, I die the next second. God protects you, darling."

"Merci, nana," Beauty plants a kiss on the nana's cheek and hugs her.

The nana lady looks saddened as the Beauty joins our group and waves back. I can't help but steal some looks at the beauty in my rear mirror. Bronze-brown curly hair crowns her head and gracefully touches her shoulders. She wears a skinny pair of jeans, a grey tight t-shirt with metallic, colorful graphics on it, and a light scarf embraces her neck, the scarf has silver strings woven into it that twinkle in the sun.

She tears a bit then engages with a small mirror in fixing her makeup. We have a quorum and we are ready to go on our ten-hour ride to Aswan.

"At any time you sense danger, feel threat, or encounter trouble, keys in the engine and head back, do you understand, Saad?" I wonder what Mr. Saqr meant by that.

The Tomb Opens

CHAPTER TWO

Aswan - Clash Intensifies

Aswan welcomes us at 8:00 PM. The arrangements have been made for the team to stay at a small hotel near the railway station called 'Hatthour'. Our feet stamp its print on the hot grounds of Aswan.

"Saad, please take me to a different hotel. I've the directions to the Mövenpick."
And who can possibly say that but lovely Salma? This Hatthour hotel in no way appreciates her style.

"Mövenpick! Good choice. This humble hotel here won't have any spa and probably features lots of mosquitoes too," mocks Ziko.

At the sound of mosquitoes, the inner corners of Salma's eyebrows meet quite far atop her forehead as if she's just seen the sad ending of a romantic movie.

"Are you thinking of another hotel too?" Salma asks Ziko.

"We're all staying here. The instructions were clear." Nadeem dictates abruptly.

"Well, I can't stay here."

"Then maybe you need to call the embassy and tell them that you quit because of a potential mosquito danger."
Nadeem replies harshly then carries his sleepy two-year old boy and heads to the lobby. He tips the guy at the door to get his suitcase.

Dr. Rashad carries his belongings and marches inside. It isn't long before Ziko gestures to Salma as if telling her --- shall we? I follow them inside wondering about my room. I've never been to a hotel before. Why should I? This is my country.

One day I'm driving my cab and killing the chewing gum out of boredom. The next day, I'm this very important person. At dinner, I rise off the table, to read the program for the first few days. It's another responsibility that Mr. Saqr has bestowed upon me.

*'Feeling good about yourself, aren't you. Well enjoy it '*حبيبي *– habiby' (my love). But remember, only the foolish thinks that privileges last,'* – Always bringing me to the harsh ground of reality, Ma. Her image faints gradually off the program paper allowing the words to re-appear and I read…

Day (1): We stroll down the streets mainly in the center area of Aswan…

"On foot?" Salma interrupts. Ziko smiles and Dr. Rashad sighs.

"Is this a joke to you?" asks Nadeem.

"Excusez-moi?"

"What are you expecting exactly? A 5-star accommodation; a luxurious trip or maybe an adventurous one where you climb mountains, ride on safari jeeps, take pictures and load them to your facebook page, just to show off and brag about it later with your snoopy friends?"

"Who gave you the right to talk to me like this?"

"This is a serious mission; it's not going to be easy, or even pleasant. Take it or leave it."

A silent cloud hovers atop our heads following Sir Nadeem's deal or no-deal statement.

"Mama!" little Bassim taps on Nadeem's arm and gets awarded a fork of pasta which his dad places carefully in his round and small mouth.

"Poor the little buddy misses his mama."
It's such an interesting pattern that every one of Ziko's comments is
followed by an aggravated sigh from Dr. Rashad.

"Please carry on, Saad," lovely Salma requests.

I clear my throat and read as follows…
"Day (1): We stroll down the streets to get a sense of the surroundings
and for the team to mark their individual focus areas
Day (2): We go to 'The Temple of Edfu'
Day (3): We visit the 'Nubian Museum'
Starting Day (4): The team will be working on their individual work
plan. I will drive the team to their chosen destinations and pick them up at
the end of the day or when they call my cell. At the end of each day, the
team will get in touch with Mr. Saqr to update him of their progress".

From the looks of the plates, Ziko and little Bassim seem to be the only
ones enjoying dinner. The rest are just staring at me, with forks in their
hands, and air filling their opened mouths. I am pretty sure that the packed
plates have gone cold and tired of waiting to be eaten. I stick the plan back
into my pocket and dig into my piled plate. This food is good, **but it stinks
compared to yours, Ma**. I can't afford nightmares tonight; I really need my
sleep.

Shortly after dawn, I find myself: fully awake, dressed and browsing the
city. It's such a beautiful puffy sunrise. A dark pink cloud stands close to the
awakening sun and another light pink wall of clouds populates the rest of the
sky. As the sun rises in pride, the clouds fade to white and the sky turns blue,
a very rich blue. With the design of buildings and streets in Cairo, it's been
so long since I last looked up and actually met the sky.

I can live here forever if it weren't for the heat that is radiating from
everywhere and making my eyes feel like grapes drying up into raisins. I
enjoy the walk then I head back to the hotel to pick-up the team.

"The Nile here is at its utmost beauty. Look how it flows through the amber desert and granite rocks."
Dr. Rashad gestures widely by his arms like he's acting a drama play on stage. But to his frustration, his poetic words get interrupted twice; once by beggars who plead for money but usually get ignored, then by some zealous voices trying to sell their merchandize. They setup their stuff neatly on two tables alongside the Nile Corniche and are calling out...

"Check this out; a great replica of Queen Hatshepsut. How about this piece of art for Tutankhamen? Enjoy the coach, and the relaxing ride. Coach Sir, only $40?"

"**Stop it!** I don't want anything and if I do I'll ask for it myself."
Dr. Rashad snaps flipping his arms like a penguin asking for help. The youths instantly freeze; one looks like the statue of 'Liberty' but with Cleopatra's head in his hand, while the other looks like 'Mother Russia' statue with an Obelisk in his hand.

Dr. Rashad's penguin-like gestures have been close enough to knock down some merchandise off one of the tables. Salma and Nadeem could care less. But Ziko's smile fades and his eyes turn serious...

"You could have just thanked the boys and told them that you aren't interested. They are young and trying to earn their living."

"They are touts harassing me. That's not earning a living."

"That's the best they know about how to earn a living in a place where new and different people pass by them every day."

"Not my problem."

"Yes, I see that. But you knocked their stuff down and you should have the courtesy to at least pick it up and pay for any damage you've caused."

"I beg your pardon. That's nonsense. Who are you to tell me what to do? I'm professor Rashad; PHD with bronze scientific prize in **research and development**."

"Well excuse me Mr. Professor, on your behalf; I'll help the boys clean up your mess."

Dr. Rashad watches Ziko go. Ziko stops after few steps and cries …"Hey Dr. Buddy, a famous poet once said… He, who can't see the beauty in anything, posses a tarred soul more than anything - Maybe you can research that."

Dr. Rashad's forehead veins pop with anger. I can see him opening his mouth to say something but then his eyes get locked at Ziko who ruffles the hair of the two boys playfully and bends to help them pick up the items strewn about on the road. He then pays the boys some money and to Dr. Rashad's surprise, buys them 2 cans of coke from their own portable fridge.

"What? Are they his cousins or something?"
Dr. Rashad mumbles then walks away. He skips dinner with us that night.

"I can't blame him." Salma tells Ziko. "A tourist asked me today… *Oh, are you Egyptian? Tell me something then, is it true that tourism in Egypt is designed to maximize extracting as much money and patience as possible from independent tourists?* You know what, I couldn't answer his question."

"Which part did you fail to answer?" Nadeem asks.

"What do you mean?" Salma inquires suspiciously.

"The 'Are you Egyptian' part or the 'money and patience' part?"
Salma's eyes narrow and her lips tighten.

"Still no answer. How about you answer yourself on that one first? I bet it'll be easier to answer others later." Nadeem teases. Salma wipes her mouth and leaves the table.

"Mama, mama," Bassim pulls Nadeem's shirt collar.

"He doesn't say much, does he? He is two years old, Right?" asks Ziko.

"Yes. Well, he was emotionally traumatized when he was 15 months. Maybe that's why his words are slowly emerging."

"Is that when he lost his mother?"

"Yes, that's when she passed away."

"Sorry buddy," Ziko pats Nadeem's shoulder.

"Mama, mama"

"Bassim needs to sleep. Good night." Nadeem carries Bassim and pats his back as he walks away.

"Do babies get traumatized at the age of 15 months? Are they really aware and can realize what dead means? I ask.

"Well, who knows what he saw, Saad? Maybe he was returning home with his father at night and then they heard a scream and his mother throws herself or gets thrown out of the balcony just so she could land at the boy's feet. I bet anyone will be traumatized by that."

I stand speechless. "Oh, come on Saad, a little suspense here and there won't hurt," Ziko humors before he disappears into his room and shuts the door.

"Nah…" I try to brush away Ziko's awfully painted picture.

The Tomb Opens

CHAPTER THREE

The Dead Awakens Passion

It's Day (2), 'The Temple of Edfu' is a 60km drive, north of Aswan. In the rear mirror I catch a glimpse of Bassim looking innocently at Nadeem's jaws as they move up and down while he teaches him how to pronounce.

"**D a d a**... come on Bassim, try it now. **D a d a**."

"M a m a" Bassim insists then giggles.

I don't have kids of my own or even a lady of my own just yet. But I haven't seen a father holding his son's hand all the time like Nadeem does. Even when he is reading him a book, he has one hand constantly holding the kid's hand. Looks like he's been so madly in love with the boy's mother.

I park. The team makes their way through the temple's entrance, while I wait in the cab.

"What are you doing here?" a police officer squints his eyes at me like he has finally found the Mafia's godfather that he has been looking for.

"I, I'm waiting ..."
"For whom?"
"For a group of people."
"Tourists?"
"No, Egyptians"
"Your id card and driver's license"
"Yes Sir," I salute politely. He checks the ids and my photo.
"Go park somewhere else. If I see you here one more time, your license will be suspended. Understood?"

"What's wrong sergeant?" Nadeem's appearance saves me.

"Is this man with you?"

"Yes, he is our driver."

"This is no place for drivers or baby sitters to be waiting. This is a touristic area."

"I don't see a sign or anything that we may have missed or violated."

The officer moves forward towards Nadeem and pushes his shoulder back with his index finger. "Here is a rule for you to remember pal: NEVER EVER talk back to a police officer or question his orders. Because if you do, your vacation here can get a lot shorter than you want. Your id!"

Nadeem reaches in his pocket and hands his id to the offensive officer.

"Lieutenant?" the officer gulps. "Ah, Sergeant Amgad Wahby - pleased to meet you, Sir."

What can I say? It is always the power game. Since the lieutenant is a higher rank than the sergeant, all of a sudden the dragon is tamed and the annoying sergeant shakes Nadeem's hand with a malleable soft tone. And I particularly enjoy it when the friendly manner extends to touch me.

"What's your name bro?"

"Huh, me? My name is Saad, Saad the driver, Sir"

"Ok, Saad, you may park on the other side, it's designated for vehicles that will be staying for few hours."

"Yes Sir," I salute again.

"Welcome to Aswan lieutenant" the sergeant, says as he walks away. Nadeem smiles and adjusts the hat on little Bassim's head.

"You might as well come and take a tour, Saad. It's causing you more trouble to wait here."

"Yes Sir"

"You don't have to call me that." Nadeem says, turns his back and with Bassim in his hand, they re-enter the temple.

I knew it; your highness turns out to be a lieutenant. I knew it.

Groups of tourists are everywhere, each with their own guide. This is incredibly weird. I hear so many languages except my mother's. Even though this is Egypt and probably all what is being said is about old Egyptians yet I can't understand anything.

I find Dr. Rashad; and by his side I stand. He stares at the wall in fascination. I bet this is an 'Awe Moment' for him, probably more than when he saw his baby walking for the first time.

حبيبي' – *habiby' (my love) – When we don't understand, we often think others are foolish, but when we do understand, we are too foolish to admit it,'* – thanks Ma.

"You know Saad - this temple covers several chapters in the book of history." I look at him, uncertain what to say so I just nod along.

"Count with me, in this one temple you see: 1) On the west side is the Mamisi, which means 'house of the divine birth'. It consists of an entrance, a court and chapel. The walls of the Mamisi are ..." *he goes on and on.*

"2) Right over here is the highest surviving Pylon in ..."
What did it survive? I ask.
"Time, Saad, it survived time," *he replies impatiently, I nod again.*

"3) As you look over at this side over there, you can appreciate the open courtyard that..."
Now that I think about it, history class was the reason I broke my ankle jumping off the school's fence.

"4) On your left is the 1st Hypostyle, which was constructed for …"
I think I went deaf, but my head is still nodding.

"5) And least but most admirable of all is the divine boat, which if you look intently is …"
This one is seriously cool.

The radius of the circle of people gathering around us keeps getting bigger. They listen to Dr. Rashad's excited tone and their heads follow where he points, some are taking pictures and others are recording what he says on their cell phones. Apparently there are some people looking for my mother's language too. Dr. Rashad acknowledges the increasing interest and raises his voice…

"The northern wall of the court shows the divine marriage of Hatthor and Horus of Behdet, which was celebrated twice every year; once at…; see how it is all still vivid and alive. Almost miraculous, isn't it?"

Dr. Rashad turns and the crowd turns; he walks and the crowd walks. I see a mama duck followed by her line of ducklings learning from her how to swim. For a second there, I think his engraved frown melted a bit under his hat.

I slowly but deliberately slip myself out like lubricating a tight ring off your finger. I find and join Ziko as he talks to a vendor at one of the souvenirs booths outside the temple.

"Nice work Osman, how much do you want for this piece?"

"It's an exact replica. It's $250."

"I love it. But see, my parents are too fond of such antiques. How old is your piece?"

Osman smiles and cocks his head… "Not that old."

"I'd pay the $250 right now for this amazing replica of Horus. But my folks might be interested in an original piece for $250,000. Do you think someone here can arrange something like that for me?"

Osman studies Ziko's face then takes a quick glimpse at me. His eyes navigate the area around us. "Why don't you come clean and say what you are really after?"

"Would you be willing to trade rusty history for fresh money?" Ziko asks, plain and straight.

"I'm not your man, pal," replies Osman.

"And who is?"

"Some people around here have more direct access to original pieces and less auditing checks. They may be interested."

"Any idea how to find them?"

"Listen, I've been around for a while. Aswan is my homeland. And I can tell that you are neither a cop, nor a buyer, not even a reporter."

Ziko scratches his chin; his smile advances then retreats. He displays a humble face with a pleading eye-look that draws the sympathy of anyone. See this professor over there." Ziko points at Dr. Rashad.
"I'm working under his supervision in a research about things that satisfy the hunger of some people who seem willing to sell the walls of their home, without a smidge of guilt."

Osman displays half a smile, puts his piece on the side and says: "The hungry don't sell the walls of their home even if they die. You know why? They can't risk being hungry AND cold. The greedy are the ones who would be willing to sell the walls of a home. But they would only sell what they don't perceive as home."

This Osman guy sounds super smart because Ziko, who outspeaks everyone, falls silent. He just smiles.

"There, I gave you the theory you were looking for, and with nothing in return. You can go and impress your professor now."

While Ziko's tongue dies, the vendor's voice rises up as clear as the sky in Aswan, to market his products…"Exact replicas, affordable prices …"

The Tomb Opens

CHAPTER FOUR

"Sauvage et Vulgaire"

The last drop of sweat I'm able to produce faints and falls dead on the ground. I hurry towards two Nubian kids laying down a couple of water bottle cartons. The words in my parched mouth halt without my permission when another police constable yells at the boys…

"Hey, if I see you here again, I'll kick your sorry butts outside this temple. Understand?"

"Cut them some slack, would you constable?"

"And who do you think you are, to stick your nose into my business?"

Once more Nadeem's id puts an end to the unneeded escalation. "Oh. Ah, Lieutenant?? Sir, these kids are harassing the tourists, Sir."

"They are offering them fresh cold beverage on a steaming hot day."

"Yes, Sir!" the constable salutes.

Nadeem leans forward and looks the kids in the eyes… "Don't run after anyone, just stay in a corner and call out for the nice, cold water bottles. People will be coming to you." The kids nod and obey.

"So are you on a 'human rights' mission, Lieutenant Sabry?" asks sergeant Wahby from behind signaling the constable to leave.

"It would be nice if power is kept tamed and is perceived as a tool to make everyone comfortable and safe; everyone, big or small, don't you think sergeant Wahby?" replies Nadeem.

"Theoretically speaking – it would be indeed nice, but police officers aren't hired to be nice. They are hired to enforce the law. The word 'enforce' comes from 'force', not nice," sleazy sergeant Wahby offers a faint sarcastic smile that beats the color and taste of mustard, then does us a favor by turning his back and leaving.

We drag our legs to the cab. Salma suggests we check out 'Philae, Temple of Isis'. All is so tired to object and too exhausted to agree. Salma compromises by promising to take a quick look while the rest of the team waits in the cab.

I accompany her. At the tickets desk, we overhear a heated argument between a couple of tourists and a boat operator...

"This is pure nonsense. After I buy your tickets to see Philae on the island, I then have to negotiate a boat across to the island. How am I supposed to see Philae if I am not at the island? What kind of deal is this? Why isn't it one package? What kind of business are you, people running here?"

"What's wrong, monsieur?" Salma barges into the argument.

"I tell you what's wrong. The boat operators know you already bought a ticket, so they gouge you as heavily as they can. And when you think you landed a deal, the fare turns from the promised $25 to $100."

"Hey copain, why don't you have une offre fixe, clear directement? Just have un prix raisonnable et bien sur, ton service will be indispensable," Salma bosses the boat operator in a mix of French, English and Arabic languages.

"The name is Captain Bakry," the boat operator lectures.

"You know what pal; we managed to latch onto a tour group that already booked a boat, so see you – never," the tourist guy teases.

"Wait a second, our sailing journey is one of its kind and we can reach a reasonable compromise," Bakry coaxes.

"Too late," replies the tourist guy.

He looks at Salma: "Thanks for trying to help, Miss. I'm sorry to say that such small victories over people like him, do boost my morale, not because I'm evil but when you have to haggle for everything from a bottle of water to your hotel room, it just ruins everything."

Then he turns at Bakry and mocks… "I wonder if it's the sun or the regret that is boiling your face now."

Salma doesn't let the awkward moment of silence last long: "Do you see le tableau maléfique that you paint pour l'Égypte? Why do you do that? You're ripping them off et ils que savent. When they leave for bon prix, you then beg pour miséricorde. Don't you have any dignity?"

I wonder if I can find a dictionary somewhere.

"You're asking me about my dignity. I embarrass you, don't I?" Bakry asks quite aggravated.

"Oui, bien sur, you do."

"Oh yeah, why? In what way are you related to me?" Bakry asks seriously yet calmly.

Salma pauses then answers: "We are both … Égyptiennes."

"Oh, really? Well, as an Egyptian, you embarrass me too."

"Excusez-moi?"

"You look like you've long fallen into a bucket of Americanizing solution that painted everything in you inside-out. I don't understand the majority of your words. You aren't even talking the language of the country you claim you belong to; and I doubt it if you know or feel proud of its culture. Rest assured lady that I'm not causing you any embarrassment, you know why? Because we are not related. Dignity? Huh?"

"Tu choisis une attitude vulgaire," Beauty says pointing her index finger at Bakry.

"You aren't the first one to say that." Bakry turns, and ignores beauty setting her face on fire.

The Tomb Opens

CHAPTER FIVE

One Family - Papa

Despite the air-conditioning running in the cab and the extreme hotness outside, yet it seems that the conversation between Salma and Bakry isn't something to be missed by the rest of the team. They've rolled down their windows, listened and witnessed the entire dramatic scene.

Salma puts on her sunglasses in prejudice, even though the sun has been gracefully saying its goodbyes for the day; marches confidently towards the cab and takes her seat. Back to the hotel I drive, only to find Mr. Saqr waiting for us in the lobby.

Mr. Saqr greets the team before calling an urgent meeting in the T.V. room. "We need to place you in an apartment," he declares.

"Excusez-moi! Who is **YOU**!" interrupts Salma.

"Allow me to finish please, will you? We don't want to draw any attention to you, all of you."

"What attention? We aren't secret service or some intelligence or spy agency trying to undergo a super dangerous and classified mission," Salma interrupts again.

"We are not Aswanians either. We'll be interacting with people here and there every day. We'll be staying for six months. We aren't running any business. So yes, this is suspicious," Nadeem explains matter-of-factly.

"And the apartment isn't?" Salma argues.

"Yes, because you can be a family considering relocating to Aswan for maybe some health reasons for their dad. A family can afford six months apartment rent, not a six months of hotel accommodation," Mr. Saqr answers so calmly. One can almost feel a cold breeze coming from his side.

"I can afford the hotel and I can be in touch with the rest of the folks every day if I need to," Salma interjects.

"It isn't really about money, Salma. It is one mission and the four of you need to stay together for safety and efficiency purposes. This isn't negotiable unfortunately," Mr. Saqr finishes off.

Salma brings her lovely lips to a firm close. They almost look like a strawberry.

"The idea of the family is perfect in this case. The four of you need to act and behave like a family; meaning no titles and as much as you possible, friendly dynamics and harmony when you interact together outside the apartment," Mr. Saqr explains.

Dr. Rashad twists and turns in his seat, knocking his cup of tea off the side table. Ziko catches the cup that spits few drops on the carpet and burns his finger. Ziko licks his finger.

"There you go dad. I am truly concerned about your health these days. You seem to knock things off more often than before. Remember what you did at the Nile Corniche with the little helpless boys and now the tea. When we return to Cairo, we are seeing a doctor and I am not hearing a NO." Dr. Rashad doesn't react to Ziko's joke, but Nadeem laughs conservatively and Salma's grimness dissolves into a sweet smile.

"Perfect. That's the family attitude you all need to advocate, great job Ziko," Mr. Saqr comments.

Day (3) looms like a wolf crawling upon his belly, in anticipation to catch his prey off guard. The tension in the air is competing with the oxygen and making it difficult for everyone to breathe. All sunglasses are casted aside and each one of the team is looking outside the window. Their eyes rather fixed and I can almost hear them saying… "Now, What?"

"We'll stop by the apartment first, I'll help you settle in, then I'll be on my way back to Cairo," announces Mr. Saqr.

It stands out as a three-storey brick building with small balconies on all its sides. We step in a very clean entrance, with floors that are recently polished yet bear no warning sign of slippery floor. The tiled walls of the entrance drop the temperature for us by at least 10 degrees Celsius.

Our apartment is on the second floor. "Welcome to your home," Mr. Saqr's footsteps precede ours and he turns the key in the lock. The door opens to a living room with a small carpet in the middle, and black and white tiles stretching all over the floor.

"Oh, finally, my dream came true," says Ziko loudly, gesturing widely with his arms while turning around slowly.

"What dream?" questions Dr. Rashad already annoyed.

"See papa, I love chess but finding a surviving partner has always been a challenge for me. But now I have the biggest chess board and we are all playing."

Little that we all know, this particular humorous line will turn out to be our destiny and only reality in the days and months to come.

"Mama," little Bassim pulls Nadeem's hand; and they go on an exploration tour around the apartment, starting by an urgent visit to the toilet.

"An apartment with two restrooms was hard to find, Salma. But there is a cleaning lady coming daily to take care of the restroom and the rest of the apartment. I understand that living with four men can be inconvenient for you but I am certain that they are all gentlemen and can make your stay rather comfortable. Let's start by giving you the option to pick your room."

"Merci," Salma walks off to check the rooms. Her face carries grimness and her cherry lips short on words.

We spend four hours in the apartment. Each one of us gets a room and empties the suitcases. Bassim is so excited; he keeps running from one room to another and Nadeem calls after him... "Bassim, knock first."

Dr. Rashad leaves for sometime and returns with a doorknob that has an embedded lock.
"Here, Salma, this is for your door. I'll fixate it for you. You can lock yourself whenever you need privacy."

Salma stands still for few seconds. She looks at the knob in Dr. Rashad's hand. She bits her lower lip for a second, looks at Dr. Rashad's face, smiles and slowly says... "Merci, ... Papa."

I suppose it is official now, two of the team calls him 'Papa'.

After Mr. Saqr leaves, they take their seats in the cab and we head for the Nubian Museum.

Bassim is cranky... "No, Mama," he keeps crying. Nadeem places him on his lap. He appears to fiddle with the keys in his pocket, turning them and rolling them in his hand, this way and that; then he pulls his hand out and surprises Bassim with a small harmonica. Bassim laughs, giggles and curls his small arms around Nadeem's neck to hug him.

"The greedy sell what they don't perceive as home. Home," Ziko muses, and mumbles repeating Osman's words.

"Do you know what home stands for ... SON?" Dr. Rashad mocks and challenges Ziko.

"I suppose,"

"I doubt it. Home means: ownership, security, warmth and peace of mind," Dr. Rashad answers with his fingers counting the list with him. I wonder how his answers are always in numbered lists.

"Ok, why would someone born in Aswan feel it isn't home? And more importantly, how can we make him feel that Aswan, the big house of temples, tombs and monuments is home? This is the worst mission ever. Civilized and productive attitude starts by liking your place and feeling that it is home, because then you'll care to be productive. Home means sense of belonging, which is Salma's mission. It seems to me that my mission is tied to Salma's," Ziko analyzes.

Dr. Rashad scratches his head…"Though highly unlikely, but you actually managed to impress me, Ziko. It turns out that God did put some effort in that head of yours after all."

Ziko smiles and Dr. Rashad continues confidently: "Let me think about it, do some research and put something into context for you."

"Thanks a lot Papa; what could I possibly do without your researching brains?"

Nadeem paints a conservative smile with closed lips, while Salma's teeth sparkle as she breaks a smile. Bassim giggles as if he understands what is being said.

In 90 minutes, the Nubian Museum stands at the horizon welcoming its visitors. I park under the designated sign and we step out of the cab, only to meet another sign that reads: "Museum is closed for the day for some maintenance and security reasons".

As we all pause for a couple of minutes thinking about all that time wasted coming here, Bassim blows hard on his harmonica. We jolt and he breaks into the cutest laugh that makes everyone laugh including Nadeem.

"He's so cute," Salma comments.

"Thanks, he looks a lot like his mother," says Nadeem in a sad tone.

Bassim extends his hand with the harmonica to me. "He wants you to play it," explains Nadeem.

I touch the harmonica; look at the beautiful solid bronze body, the holes opening in pride as if daring me to touch them. I take a deep breath, and I start streaming a current of air inside them. I am so liking what I am hearing.

'That's every mother's wish, for her son to be a musician composer even if he is shoeless' – Thank god, I was starting to get worried about you, Ma. *'Always around* 'حبيبي *– habiby' (my love)*.

"Saad, you may keep the harmonica," Nadeem tells me.

The Tomb Opens

CHAPTER SIX

Mother Beauty Arrives

The evening blows on us some nice breeze, something exciting will happen tonight. I've always had this hunch. *"Yeah Right"*, hey Ma! I guess my hunch failed me this time.

Dr. Rashad calls the first team meeting. Everyone gather in the living room. They take their seats. Dr. Rashad stands outside the seating area. He has a flip chart and a thin metal rod.

"Oh, it's a class not a meeting. How exciting! I must have misunderstood then," Ziko teases.

Dr. Rashad starts: "If we want to talk about: belonging and productivity, then we'll have to start with OWNERSHIP. I belong to what I own. I am productive because I care, and I care because I own. Got it?"

"Bummer – I don't have a notebook to take notes. Is there a DVD or mp3 version of this lecture that we can maybe watch or listen to later?" Ziko mocks and for the first time ever Dr. Rashad ignores. It looks like the burning sun in Aswan has melted his angry reflexes or maybe his immune system has grown to repel the Ziko effect.

Dr. Rashad goes on, "The tough part is: if I'm to believe that a place is my OWN, my voice will be heard in it. My needs will be acknowledged in it. I will be respected in it. I won't be shooed like a herd of small animals, or annoying bugs. Yes, there will be rules, ones that I've come to learn the value of, or ones that I am in agreement with because I was taught the sense behind having them."

Dr. Rashad finishes and his eyes land on Nadeem. Ziko exhales a smile.

"You're referring to the police officers and security representatives who are scramming the locals away, limiting their existence in the temples and affecting their business."

"It is an attitude Nadeem; Attitude instilled in the brains of the law-enforcement personnel, as the right way to do things. It is an attitude that is quickly turning into a behavior and sooner than desired will be a culture. It is way dangerous than it looks. But yeah, for the sake of this conversation and this small group and not to overwhelm your brains here, sure, your example is a valid and obvious issue, Nadeem," Dr. Rashad says.

"Come-on Dr. Buddy, are you saying that focusing on those who steal the monuments and sell them abroad, or concentrating on any potential terrorist threat, is more important than running after the kids selling water bottles with a club? Come-on!" mocks Ziko.

"I understand your point Dr. Rashad and that's why I'm taking care of such attitude. It lies within the responsibilities of my mission," affirms Nadeem confidently. I dismiss the urge to salute.

"How – exactly – are you taking care of this? You're advising the authorities not to misuse their power by flashing your id to them?" Salma confronts Nadeem then changes her tone into a deep and gruff voice…
"Hey, don't misuse your power, fellow officer. Don't you know who I am? I'm the LIEUTENANT. I use my power to make you not use yours. Understood?"
Then in a rather frightened yet obedient tone she replies to her own question:
"Sir, yes Sir."

Dr. Rashad looks interested. Ziko tries to hide his mouth that is opening widely in an ear-to-ear grin. I find it amusing too. Nadeem's gaze locks on Salma's for few seconds. His jawbones pulse like he instantly chewed on a gum. He exhales half a smile. The anticipation of his reaction stays hot and beating until he freezes it by choosing not to answer.

Dr. Rashad ends the lingering tense moment by clearing his voice: "Back to ownership, I have some ideas that can help you, Ziko, get started."

"I'd be willing to help too, Ziko, I am not hiding behind a badge, so my help can actually be effective and makes more sense," adds Salma, stepping gracefully yet intentionally on Nadeem's nerves.

Dr. Rashad joins me later, on the balcony of the living room. "You like watching the moon, or the stars better, Saad?"

"I like the full moon, but I also like looking at the sky during a blackout."

"Why blackout?"

"Because, the tiny stars illuminate the entire sky, despite the fact that the sky is thick and dark, like my mother's velvety dress that she wore to both weddings and funerals. The stars look like sparking diamonds to me. I haven't actually seen a real diamond before. But you hear people talking about how sparkly diamonds are. Anyway, when electricity contributes, the stars tend to shy away and it's up to the moon to stand the ground. But it only happens when the moon is full like tonight. You must think that I am crazy."

"Not at all."

"Talking about crazy, I feel that the moon in Aswan is bigger than it is in Cairo. Is that even possible, Dr. Rashad?"

"You are not crazy, Saad. You are genuinely observant and your logic is straight and simple. The way I see it is: the sky that looks like your mother's dress is our life filled with challenges. The stars are us, mankind. The shining power in each star is each individual's ability or gift or strength, which they are born with. When we operate together, we shine more and bring light to the universe. Electricity is the corruption, or human demons that want to turn off the stars, but camouflages as a helping tool, until we grew dependant on," Dr. Rashad elaborates and surprisingly I find myself catching-up with his train of thoughts.

"What about the moon?" I dare to ask, following along.

"The moon is our will to defend our existence."
Dr. Rashad drinks the last sip of his tea and continues: "Say what you said to people, they might laugh but not call you crazy. Try saying what I said to people, even those who call themselves educated, and you'll be granted the forever-insane label. And yes, Saad, the moon is bigger in Aswan, you know why? Because the possibilities in Aswan are bigger."

I stare at Dr. Rashad for few seconds. This man is a well. You draw out of it and it just comes out with more.

"Oh, I didn't realize someone is out here…" interjects Nadeem as he steps onto the balcony.

"Actually I was about to ask Saad if he could kindly make me another cup of tea. Would you like to join us for a warm cup of tea under the moonlight?"

"Sure, why not?" replies Nadeem.

I return with three cups of tea, garnished by some fresh green mint leaves. The mint spreads its aromatic smell everywhere while teasing the red boiling tea by adding a strong flavor to its bitter taste. Nadeem is in the middle of his conversation…

"It's not that I want to, but that's what I know. It's like you are a carpenter but the tool that you really use is the hammer. People say: we need you on a job Mr. Carpenter. I say: sure thing, I'll bring my hammer. No, bring something else; this job needs a carpenter but not necessarily a hammer, they explain. I am willing to take the job but hammering is all I know."

"I understand" Dr. Rashad says, "But maybe you need to allow yourself to think outside the box. It is hard especially for an officer who is used to command and obey commands…"

A knock on the door followed by Salma's instant happy scream… "MOM…" interrupts Dr. Rashad's train of thoughts and brings the three of us to the living room. We see Salma hugging an older version of hers.

"Mother, please meet: Dr. Rashad, Nadeem, Ziko, Saad, et bon Bassim."

"Enchanté," says Salma's mother.

Salma takes her mother's hand and they walk to Salma's room… "How did you know I am here?"

"Un détective privé"

"What?"

"Qui sont tous ces hommes? Et dont l'enfant est-ce? Me répondre maintenant jeune dame," the ladies close the door but it looks like it's going to be a long night of chatting.

"That's it, the second we return back to Cairo, I am learning Italian," Ziko says painting his face serious.

"This isn't even Ita..." Dr. Rashad starts. "You know, it isn't even worth it." He finishes off, heads to his room and slams the door.

Ziko laughs lightly and then cries: "*Buona Notte* (Good night), Papa."

The Tomb Opens

CHAPTER SEVEN

Something Fishy

The night roars away and Day (4) opens its sleepy eyes as we gather in the cool entrance. Ziko is late.

"I'm a very light sleeper; and since Ziko's room is next to mine, I'm pretty sure he was up till very late. Doing what? I'll never be able to predict," Dr. Rashad says.

Few minutes later, a fried version of Ziko comes down the stairs carrying a huge hockey-sized bag. "Good morning," he greets us enthusiastically.

I'm not hallucinating when I say that I've actually caught a hint of a smile on Dr. Rashad's face. Bassim points at Ziko and giggles.

"Ziko, what are you doing?" asks Salma

"I'm a local Aswanian now, A Nubian, if you will," he answers proudly.

At the Nubian museum, we all stand and watch Ziko as he pulls out some Bristol boards and stand-up frames from his huge bag. The boards have images and pictures of Nubians, of some monuments, and of some Aswan attractions. Some of the images are hand-drawn while others are pasted pictures.

"Wow, Ziko, *c'est formidable* – this is amazing. How and when did you do all that?" Salma asks.

"I went down to few hotels last night; checked the lobby for some postcards, and picked the things that represented Aswan and the Nubian culture. I borrowed Dr. Rashad's laptop; looked-up some other images off the Internet, but with the lack of a printer, I found no choice but to draw them myself. Now it's show time!"

We step back, as Ziko's voice rings loud and clear…

"مرحباً في أسوان" – Welcome to Aswan,"

He starts in Arabic with a Nubian accent then repeats in English.

"Aswan's inhabitants are we, the Nubians. We are believed to be the first human race on earth, and most of our customs and traditions were adopted from the ancient Egyptians. Get to know us and you'll find that Nubians are the most hospitable, friendly and loyal people you can ever meet around the world. Welcome to our museum, don't forget to ask and learn about our culture, our traditions and our rescue campaign. Dive in the history that our great-great-grand ancestors created. Welcome to our land, it's good to have you over."

"He is *brillant* – brilliant," Salma compliments.

"He is an actor, and he'll get himself in trouble because he demands attention," Nadeem shakes his head in dismay.

"*Tu as besoin de te relacher* – you need to loosen-up a bit, this isn't *les services secrets* – secret services, it is creative and fun," Salma toggles between languages. It is amazing how she does it.

"You'll be surprised," Nadeem corrects.

People pile around Ziko; all listen and nod, then make their way inside the museum. Some Nubians gather too and I can see smiles breaking on their lips in pride. Bassim and I play with the harmonica, whenever Nadeem goes and talks to any security guard or police officer that tries to annoy Ziko or interrupt his show.

"Sergeant Wahby, we don't want to violate any rule, or even request an exceptional treatment of any kind. If there is any paper work that we need to file, we're happy to do so. We're willing to communicate and work out an agreement," says Nadeem firmly but sincerely. Sergeant Wahby doesn't answer; he just nods briefly and leaves.

At home, Dr. Rashad wears the chef hat by assigning dinner tasks to everyone. They are in a good mood, so they follow along. Ziko is barbecuing the chicken on the balcony. Salma is setting the table. In the kitchen Dr. Rashad is boiling the pasta, I am washing the vegetables; Nadeem is cutting up some watermelon.

"Nadeem, I noticed that Bassim doesn't eat certain food," Dr. Rashad says.

"Yeah, well, he is only two. He'll eat more as he grows up."

"True, but you need to give him a taste of different things, so he doesn't grow-up picky. I have some healthy kids' friendly recipes. I can make some for you to try first. If you like them, you can introduce them to Bassim."

"Thanks a lot Dr. Rashad. No need for trouble."

"Oh, it is no trouble at all, it is my pleasure."

I am starting to miss the grumpy, complainer's flavor of Dr. Rashad's. This friendly manner sounds odd to me and doesn't quite suit him.

'Focus 'حبيبي – habiby' (my love), you're almost squishing the tomatoes. It is hot in Aswan and the tomatoes are ripe' – Thanks, Ma.

At the dinner table, Salma's mother joins but she brings her own hotel-made food. Her mouth hardly opens and she makes a lot of noise with her shiny, heavy utensils. Nadeem tastes Dr. Rashad's special healthy dish. He doesn't seem to like it much, but he smiles politely and takes few more spoons out of curtsey. Bassim extends his fork to taste it but Nadeem quickly pushes the plate away.

The next morning, Dr. Rashad cooks another special healthy dish. Nadeem reluctantly pushes the second spoon-full in his tight mouth. He forces the food down his throat, but his throat objects and throws it back up. Nadeem covers his mouth with his hand, and rushes to the restroom. We hear his throw-up melody loud and clear.

Bassim extends his fork to try the healthy food, but it's Dr. Rashad who pushes the dish away from him this time. He clearly doesn't want Bassim to have any. I can almost see him smiling with a dash of evilness. Something is fishy. Could it be that papa isn't much of a good man after all?

The Tomb Opens

CHAPTER EIGHT

Nubian Museum

The very next day, the Nubian museum remains our destination. Ziko does a fine job. He becomes eloquent in his presentations; and the switch between Arabic and English is smoothly and seamlessly done that one could literally hear just the one language that he understands.

I see sergeant Wahby watching and giving those brief conservative smiles. Words spread and Osman the antique crafter finds himself a place among the crowd as well.

"Whenever you've a break, I'd like to talk to you," Osman tells Ziko.

Salma adjusts the boards on the frames, hands Ziko lots of water bottles to keep his voice moist and going. Dr. Rashad takes notes. Nadeem keeps his eyes open; his head literally turns 360 degrees, yet he still manages to keep playing with little Bassim.

"Listen, do you think you can run the show for a couple of hours until I come back?" Ziko asks Salma.

"*Moi* – Me? I'd love to help. But I am not sure I can. It looks like it requires a lot of coordination between the talking and adjusting the boards. I am accustomed to power point but I am afraid this manual process, *pas pour moi* – not for me."

Ziko masterfully filters a lot of Salma's words. He leans the stack of boards on the wall behind him.
"Sure, you can. Come on, give it a try and remember: Arabic is your language, friendly is your attitude; hospitality and pride are your qualities. Right Dr. Rashad?"

"Excellent Ziko, you learn quickly."

"Yeah, the smartest of my brothers, is who I am."

Salma pauses in hesitation, then straightens her back and looks around. Luckily there is no audience at the moment; she gracefully draws a smile on her face... "مرحباً في أسوان – *Mesdames, Messieurs, Bonjour et Bienvenue au Aswan*"

"Oh, I'm stronger in French," Salma clarifies.

Ziko pauses a little... "Great, we'll be talking to our French visitors then."

Ziko leaves Salma in charge. I can see her struggling with keeping one whole sentence in Arabic but amazingly she is more fluent in French. I wonder how this is even possible. Didn't her mother yell at her in Arabic when she was little? Didn't the neighbors' dad swear at his wife in Arabic? Didn't she listen to songs and watch movies that are composed and produced in Arabic? I guess not. But she's trying hard.

Since it isn't my mother's language, I feel bored, so I leave and walk around. And there he is, Ziko, talking to Osman.

"Osman, you're really gifted. Your antique replicas are pieces of art. How about you setup next to my show? And I am pretty sure your work will wow the crowd."

"Listen Ziko, my setup at the temple is promising paradise gates for me; a lot more than I've dreamed to earn, a fortune if you will."

"These gates of paradise, are they opening just now? Why now?"

"You have to play by the rules and I did. I setup, I watched, I realized, and I didn't blab. Bottom line, I proved to be a candidate. Leaving means declining to cooperate and opportunities like this come once in one's life. Sharing with you can actually jeopardize such opportunity. The reason I am talking to you is, because I know you belong to the same life-school I belong to, and you'd understand that it is better for each one of us to stay and play in his area of focus."

Ziko smiles briefly then leans forward, looks into Osman's eyes and lowers his voice…

"Yes, I belong to the same school and trust me Osman, going for an alliance with some guards or officers, businessmen and wealthy buyers is like entering a Mafia web. Yes, it can open paradise gates for you in terms of money but you won't be at peace with yourself. Yes, it is a daring adventure, and everyone is doing it, and yeah, it is wrapped in an 'OPPORTUNITY' ribbon, but because you are an artist, you'll regard yourself a mugger who needs to steal Nefertiti's head and ship it offshore to who ever can pay more. You can still sell Nefertiti's head but the one that you made. It won't reward you the same amount of money, but it's by far much more rewarding to the artist inside you, and it isn't at all risky. Think about it, Osman. You are born a crafter, use such talent, other doors will open for you, I assure you."

Osman's pause doesn't last long…"Would you help me carry my stuff, and bring it over?"

"Right this second, let's go." Ziko takes off with Osman.

Osman looks worried and hesitant. And even though Ziko has sounded like a courageous hero to me, the look in his eyes casts defeat and shame.

The Tomb Opens

CHAPTER NINE

Ziko

After dinner we gather in our living room. Salma's mother is at her spa appointment at Mövenpick. She spends most of her time there. Every one of us now has a good olive tan, even Salma who keeps spraying Bassim and herself with sun block.

"It wasn't in the plan to talk Osman into choosing a different career path. You want to tell us why you did it or how this is serving your mission?" asks Dr. Rashad.

Ziko's smile fades gradually. The look in his eyes suggests that his life has just flashed in front of him.

"Fellows, let not my well-groomed appearance, fool thy,"
They laugh and Dr. Rashad smiles. If Ziko doesn't start off with a joke, who will?

"I am thirty years old. Actually just for the records, today is my birthday. I come from a very humble family; one of those neighborhoods where the lack of shoes doesn't prevent kids from playing street soccer all day long. We would eat and drink anything, some days we won't have anything-solid coming down our stomachs but because we played and ran, we didn't care.

Besides soccer, we all had one thing in common: we didn't see but grimness on our fathers' faces. Staying in school was a privilege, only for the lucky. Kids in such neighborhoods pleaded to remain in school, because the other alternative was to work at a very young age in anything and everything, basically according to what your body can tolerate. It was a dull future as we saw it. Our fathers lived it and we were destined to follow through; one of the reasons we kept kicking really hard at the ball.

I overheard my father numerously explaining to my mother how the pain was eating him alive as hopelessness leapt and caught up with him every way he turned, fighting every attempt he made, determined to suffocate every hope he had to provide us with a better standard of living.

And please don't get me wrong; I am not complaining that we didn't have a big T.V. or a comfortable car or didn't get the chance to enjoy a relaxing vacation at the Riviera in the summer time."

Ziko pauses for very long couple of minutes, he doesn't look down. I catch his eyes glistening, his facial expressions masterfully and quickly drawing the lines of suppressed rage looks. He collects himself, and with a higher tone he paints his vivid picture...

"I didn't see water coming down tapes **EVER** in our tiny apartment. We used **BUCKETS**. The light in the lamps faded and flickered 60 times per minute. Have you ever felt the fear of getting blind, **EVERY** night? That flickering was because of the lengthy wires that we used to steal electricity from the closet neighborhoods, which unlike us were destined to have electricity. I hated the flickering but the alternative was pitch-black darkness.

Almost everyone in my neighborhood practiced panhandling except those foolish ones who thought they were better than that. I was one of those. I wanted money and I wanted it bad but I wanted people to offer it to me. Talented, I regarded myself as; therefore begging and I couldn't be buddies.

And down the alleys, we kept on playing and kicking the ball hard. We dreamed to be famous soccer players, wealthy and lovable. It sounded possible and it spoke to the passion in our hearts.

I was born with the curse of noticing others. Why is it a curse? Because what I saw wasn't pretty. From the age of five, I witnessed old women calling out after people:
"Sir, can you please help me", "Mme, can you please spare some change".

On a couple of occasions, I extended my small hand with the nickels I received as an allowance. Some of those women accepted it with a flood of tears; others shook their heads, smiled and refused.

Those beggar-women would be aching of blisters on the soles of their dry bleeding feet, unable to walk yet limping through their pain, asking passengers here and there, in hopes for merciful hearts. Passengers were disgusted at such women. Some would throw some nickels and others would refuse to even **LOOK** at their condition.

There is a difference between looking and actually seeing. When you look, there is a chance you can see. But, **NOOOO!!** Those women were rid that chance.

Pedestrians looked embarrassed to be in neighborhoods where panhandlers existed. They would frown or whistle or talk over their phone, speed up and leave without looking back. Car drivers pausing for traffic would roll-up their windows and turn on the music louder.

The intent was not to hear the begging, because then they might listen to the cries and pain underneath it, which could lead to sympathy, and then to public sentiment. But sentiment wasn't for the poor or the needy. Now you know why it was a curse? I envied those who blocked the scenes or images they didn't like. But, how? How do I turn my eyes off? And if I can, can I also turn my ears off?

I saw kids being yelled at for asking for a nickel to eat a sandwich, when the food thrown in the garbage bins on the streets wasn't enough to feed them all. I observed men been cursed at, for being homeless, **AS IF IT WAS BY CHOICE.**"

Ziko's voice softens…

"I didn't **JUST** see or observe or witness. Those people were my neighbours and my community. Those were people I grew up to play with, to love, and to share laughs with. Those who were being treated as society viruses were those whom I belonged to. As years rolled, and their conditions didn't ameliorate, I just kept wondering… Oh, god, is there nothing more anyone can do?

That's why I grew up appreciating everything my parents were trying to put up with that saved me the begging and the asking. They accepted charity all year long but luckily didn't set-up in a corner with opened palms.

I promised myself never to continue living a humble life; never to bring kids to the world if I can't provide them with a decent life. The one heart that shared this dream with me was my neighbour and potential bride, Rubab. In neighborhoods like mine, love was the only rescue.

My parents' main investment in me was education. They followed up with me and not once did they ignore any of my absence attempts from school. I grew up to be a hard worker. Yet I kept jumping from one job to another. They all simply said: "Oh, you've been replaced!" The replacements weren't based on qualifications but on relationships, business affairs, and common interests.

I accepted such dynamic change with sportsmanship, convincing myself that it was real life for everyone. Until the day when Rubab, my childhood and youth sweetheart, got engaged to a rich guy...
"Oh, you've been replaced!" yet again.
Common interests penetrated through **my** personal life. My lady had an interest in a better life style and the rich guy had an interest in beauty. They sealed the deal and Ziko's contract came to an end."

Ziko sighs. Salma's sympathetic eyes refuse to let go of Ziko. Nadeem shows no emotion as usual and Dr. Rashad shakes his head as the story progresses.

"I worked three months for free as a reimbursement for the money I needed to burry my parents with. They both died on the same week Rubab got married, by god knows what disease. Well, an affordable and good doctor was a fictitious character, one to be watched only on movies, just like batman and superman.

But please don't feel bad for me. My life had turned 180 degrees, because I forced it to. See from that time on, my motto in life became deceit and cheating. My creativity came into play. I enjoyed the outcome and took pride in my well-done job.

I camouflaged; shed crocodile tears; cheated; disguised in: women, fat retarded youths, old men, psychics, gurus, and religious figures. I committed frauds of almost all kinds. My dream came true and people offered me money, willingly and with a smile, sometimes even begged me to accept it. Ironic, isn't it? One thing I didn't do though was that I never caused a woman or a female any harm. I just saw my mother in all women."

Oh, thank god, I don't see my mother in all women.

"To be a big shark was never a dream of mine, nor was it simply attainable. I was just one smart and crafty survivor fish but at the end just a fish not a shark. I lacked the cold-blood, the dead heart and the sharp teeth of a shark. So fact is, sooner or later I will be eaten. That's when I decided to immigrate, driven by the desire to be irreplaceable, safe and respected."

Ziko pauses, and sips some water. All eyes are on him.

"Osman is my exact replica, only ten years ago. It always amazed me before, how generously the evil can lend a hand and pulls more supporters to their side while the good's hand is always short, pre-occupied and negligent of those in need for a rescue.

I wish I can help Osman and people like him but here I am, the deceiving, manipulative and disgusting Ziko. I talked to him into rejecting a chance that will earn him more money. I based my logic on his talent. I used his passion to drive him where I want him to be. Why? Because this will help my mission and it will grant me a Visa. And yes, I refuse to think about what he'll do after I am out of here, because I am not thinking of him as a human being, but rather a rescue tube.

Don't judge me folks, for '**Life**' is my role model and that's what '**Life**' in beloved Egypt had taught me. This is who I am – this is who I am. "

Ziko buries his face in the palms of his hands for a couple of seconds, lifts his face up, a dreadful look coloring his sweaty face, he drops his rounded head, his chin fails to touch his Adam's apple because it is well sunken in his double chin. He heads towards the door and leaves. The room falls silent. The lights are turned off. All tired bodies find their beds and retire their thoughts for the day; all but Ziko. He has relived his entire life with us tonight; and no say about when he'll be able to retire his thoughts.

The Tomb Opens

CHAPTER TEN

If you can't beat them, join them

The sun generously baths Aswan's roads on Day (6).
"Today, we'll split the efforts. Ziko will maintain his show appearance at the museum, while Salma rents a felucca for the day. Nadeem will accompany Ziko while we accompany Salma," Dr. Rashad directs and the team doesn't argue.

"Salma, remember, think first, pick your words in your head, then talk slowly to avoid the auto bi-lingual translator that confuses the people you talk to," Dr. Rashad advises.

Salma blushes and doesn't look happy.

"Salma, you are a grown-up person and you understand I am saying this to help you. So quit getting offended," Dr. Rashad says and turns his back without waiting for Salma to respond.

"D'accord – Agreed, Oops!"

At the deck, there are several feluccas. Each felucca has on it the name of its captain: 'Captain Moustache', 'Captain Hook', 'Captain Waves', 'The Pirate', and 'Horus – Captain Bakry'. Salma walks by 'Horus', Bakry's felucca; ignores him and pays for a sail ride with Captain Moustache.

During the 60 minutes tour, Captain Moustache gets high then sings loudly… "She'll be smoking down the mountain when she comes, she'll be smoking down the mountain when she comes…" Salma is appalled. I find it funny though.

Salma gets us another tour with Captain Hook. In his 60 minutes tour, he is operating the felucca while his assistant sings: "Row, Row, Row your boat, gently down the stream…" over and over and over again. Lucky most of the passengers have earphones and the rest are talking to each other, because to me it feels as if I've landed in a beehive, head first and I seriously consider jumping in the river.

Bakry offers a 90 minutes tour. We pass by him twice. The first time, he is holding on to the mast, pointing at the horizon and talking to his passengers. The second time, his crew is drumming some Nubian tunes. From afar it looks entertaining.

Salma fights with her pride for some time before she finally takes the steps towards Bakry's felucca.

"Good morning Captain Bakry. We'd like to rent your felucca for the day. We'll be running the business and we need you to operate it. We'll need your entertaining crew as well. Are you interested?" Salma talks fully Arabic.

"For the whole day, I'll take $300 flat rate and 40% of what each customer will pay. Deal?"

"Deal," Salma extends her hand and shakes it firmly with Bakry. The first tour is just for the three of us. Dr. Rashad keeps pointing at stuff and telling Salma what to say and how to say it.

The second tour, Salma calls out…"Nice Felucca ride; flip back through the book of history, enjoy the tranquility and charm of authentic Egypt." She talks in Arabic and in French… "$30 per head for a 90 minutes ride."

The felucca fills up quickly. Salma's voice rise: "Welcome to our graceful felucca. We'll be cruising along the islands of the Nile. Over there, look and watch how the people of Aswan go about their daily routines on the Nile. You'll meet farmers operating simple irrigation equipment. You'll spot groups of farm laborers tending for their domestic animals. You'll be charmed by children running playfully and enjoying the river."

Salma does well. But I can sense her anxiety building up. I pull the harmonica out my pocket and I start playing softly. I look at the rich blue sky and I don't realize it when I start singing along with the crew some Nubian songs; I love the rhythm. The crew does some awesome drumming. Everyone starts tapping their feet and applauding along.

"It has been a magical ride. We're coming again. Thanks," people greet us.

Dr. Rashad takes notes as usual, but to my surprise in the following tours, he sticks his notebook in his back pocket and tapes the ride on his video camera.

It is our seventh and last tour for the day. I am very exhausted but I've really enjoyed it. The sun has already set. Bakry gestures to one of his crew, who then illumes some campfire on the boat.

"Wow, fireside entertainment. We feel like we're having a real adventure, sharing a truly memorable experience, that is authentically Egyptian," one of the guests raves and everyone nods, mumbles and agrees.

Bakry smiles in pride. Salma's eyes don't reflect excitement or happiness, but a rather empty and shallow look, as if her mind is in a whole other place, and her eyes are a pair of glossy glass with no life.

"Merci, Captain Bakry, we truly enjoyed it," says Salma.

"You're welcome," he shakes hands with Salma, deposits the money in his pocket then calls his crew to clean up and close for the day.

The Tomb Opens

CHAPTER ELEVEN

Poisoned Lesson

I'm about to drop dead but I drag myself and join the team in the living room. Ziko narrates how his show has gone well:
"With Osman's antiques, your memory of Aswan will never vanish. His masterpieces have a legend: they'll bring you back to Egypt. We welcome you in Aswan and we want to see you again. Check Osman's booth, his work is a true compliment to the Egyptian history."

Ziko explains how his words have brought lucrative profit to Osman on his first day at the doors of the museum.

"How about you, Nadeem?" Dr. Rashad follows with the next name on his list.

"I wasn't presented by any legal reason that requires Ziko or Osman to leave their spots. They aren't too close to the museum, yet they are still visible. They don't run after tourists or bug them. Osman has a board with an index of his merchandise and the cost of each piece to steer clear from any manipulation accusation by Wahby and his men. Having said that though, I know that it won't be long before Osman will be removed. Wahby is annoyed and suspicious. We may need to think of a different approach, if you, Ziko, think that what you are doing is actually helping your mission progress. Do you believe that it is?"

"My mission is the civilized and productive attitude. I need more Osman(s) and I am golden. Thanks anyway, Nadeem, I'll think of what else I can do," Ziko answers, brushing away Nadeem's concerns.

Nadeem then directs his words to Salma: "On a different note, there is a Global Summit taking place here tomorrow. Leaders from the Middle East, Europe, America and some United Nations folks are coming to town.

They'll be staying and meeting at the Old Cataract Hotel, it's now called Sofitel Hotel. Anyway, due to the extensive security measures, I don't think it's a good idea for Salma to continue her felucca activities, because it is in the same area."

"Well, has anything been announced? Does this mean no feluccas will operate during the summit? Because this will be crazy. Tourists come for such activities. Are you telling me that tourism will be put on hold until the summit is over? Why do they hold it here anyway?" Salma's series of questions run fluently then halt all together.

Nadeem sighs, his nostrils flare and the air in his mouth fills up into a ball shaped mouth until it is finally released, turning the ceiling fan a bit in the clockwise direction.

"Are you asking or arguing? Summits are big deal; and No, they don't walk around announcing that tourism will be put on hold. But this doesn't mean that there are no security measures that will be put in effect as needed."

"Let's not go then, Salma," Salma's mother advises.

"If the felucca operators are going, I don't see why I can't."

"Have you heard about the G20 that took place in Toronto few days ago? During such events, safety and security of international leaders and presidents is the number one priority. Police forces are empowered. Mischievous acts are anticipated. There is no time to check and double check. Guards are instructed not to react to trouble but to proactively prevent it. Laws are formed overnight and applied in the morning. You should not go," Nadeem enforces.

"Merci, for the warning. But I'm a big girl and I can take care of myself. Advices make me irritated, let alone warnings. Merci, again. Have a nice evening," Salma walks off to her room.

"She is a bit stubborn, that's all," mother beauty comments.

"I suggest you accompany her, tomorrow," Dr. Rashad tells her.

"Who? Me? Well, may I have all your cell phone numbers then, just in case we needed to get in touch with you?"
I write all cell phones on a paper for her. She types them on her cell phone then follows Salma to her room.

"They think that if they went to school, they can understand what safety and security means," Nadeem mumbles then walks off to check on Bassim. Bassim has been playing with Ziko: cars, catch the ball, and hide and seek.

"He is fast asleep. He is one active and funny young fellow. I'll head for the shower then go out for an urban walk," Ziko says.

From the balcony, I see Ziko leaving. Nadeem joins me. "It's nice out here. Oh, this boiled mint is good, I hope it fixes my broken colon," Nadeem says as he gulps the boiled mint.

"Hey, Nadeem, drink this, it'll make you feel better" says Dr. Rashad as he steps into the balcony.

"Oh, No, No, I am good with the boiled mint."

"The boiled mint wouldn't do you any good, trust me. Drink this."

"See, Dr. Rashad, I don't mean to offend you and I know you meant well. But the healthy recipes aren't working for me. If anything they are draining my energy due to consecutive episodes of throw-up and diarrhea. I am returning back to my unhealthy diet and Bassim will eventually grow up and eat more. So, thanks, but No, thanks."

Dr. Rashad laughs. Since this is no time for laughing, I look at him intently and as I do so, his mouth grows wider, his laughter becomes louder, his eyes look wickeder and he turns into one psycho maniac.

'Wake-up 'حبيبي *– habiby' (my love), ' –* thanks, Ma. I rub my eyes and try to catch-up.

Dr. Rashad looks normal again; he puts his natural frown back on: "Sorry, I had to laugh because that's the typical thing you'd see in a movie, and I was trying to be funny."

He probably senses how weird we think he is. So he cuts his pause. "Anyway, you are right, Nadeem. Your stomach couldn't handle the healthy food because it wasn't healthy at all."

I don't understand why he keeps pausing. What kind of reaction is he expecting from us? He cuts his un-needed pause one more time.

"See, I added a mixture of Asian spices that shouldn't be added together in one recipe. The throw-up and diarrhea are normal side effects. Have you experienced any burn when you pee yet?"

"Why would you do that? And you wanted Bassim to eat it?" Nadeem asks, his eyebrows collecting all the hair possible and forming one serious knot at the top of his nose.

"Oh, No, No, I would have never let Bassim try that. See, Nadeem, when police forces use power: normal, extensive, or exaggerated – they claim that they do so because it's needed for national safety. Just like when I claimed to have some recipes for Bassim's safety.

I hurt you, you stopped trusting me but you still don't know what a healthy recipe is and whether or not you actually need it. Security officers don't share the cases and scenarios. They don't educate civilians. They believe they know better and they believe that's enough. They don't even announce the accountability and responsibility when something goes wrong.

With force, corruption grows and injustice dominates but with education, the foundation gets stronger.

Your mission, Nadeem, isn't to exert more power over the powerful. Your mission is to educate the powerful on how to use their power, which we'll bring us back to education. That's the point I wanted to make."

Nadeem's jaw is hanging open just like mine. He stares at Dr. Rashad for few minutes, his veins popping with anger, his hands roll into fists, his knees are a bit bent and his legs are apart.

"You almost poisoned me, to prove your point?"

"It was no poison, I swear; just some unfriendly spices that irritate the digestion. But its effect isn't long term. You stop the spices, you are healed; unlike all the torture and physical abuse that the police forces do with the civilians behind bars before and after the court trials. Listen, Nadeem, you are as stubborn as Salma and this was the only way, you'd consider my theory."

"You are a crazy old man and I can get you arres…" Nadeem snaps then swallows the rest of his sentence.

"Arrested. I know you can," Dr. Rashad completes it for him.

Nadeem's stormy reddish look turns blue as if he's been splashed in the face with very cold bucket of water. He turns and stomps away.

"Saad, will you please make him a large cup of tea with lemon before he goes out."

"Did he say he's going out?"

"He needs to do some serious thinking. Just make him the tea; it'll make his stomach feel a lot better, besides you are maybe the only one he still doesn't distrust. See, police officers either distrust or not distrust. Anyway, just do it, please."

I turn to leave.

"Well, that's what a papa would do… teach his son with evidence and proofs," Dr. Rashad mumbles to himself.

This mission is growing dangerously than I have anticipated. Is it time to leap yet? I wonder unaware of the pain that tomorrow beholds for me.

The Tomb Opens

CHAPTER TWELVE

Ouch...

Day (7) promises to take us aboard another cruise. I see the Nile River in Aswan like a youthful virgin lady. Fully aware of her beauty, she walks in pride and joy. All around is dreaming to win her. The light breeze extends its fingers in shyness and tickles its waters gently as if politely begging for a charming smile to illuminate the day.

"We'd like to rent your boat again for the day Captain Bakry. But we'd like to stop by a Nubian village for 30 minutes every tour. Is this OK with you?" Salma asks rather politely.

"As long as you'll pay me, I'm good," replies Bakry blunt and cold.

"Good, please affix this sign for us" Salma asks.
The sign says:
   Horus Voyage – A Truly Authentic Egyptian Nile Adventure
   Ride is 120 minutes
   Included - 30 minutes visit to a Nubian Village
   Price = $40 /adult, $25 /child
   Maximum Capacity = 15 passengers
   Tour runs every 180 minutes

Captain Bakry reads, looks at Salma with a smile that says with a hint of sarcasm: "yeah, right."

"This will give us some time to clean the boat and rest after each tour. When you set your terms in advance and respect them, everyone will respect you," Salma teaches Bakry. She looks at Dr. Rashad. He nods in approval, then waves to us and leaves.

"Whatever," Bakry replies

"Be our guest, on a complimentary short camel caravan to a near-by Nubian Village for tea with the local Aswanians. We'd like to extend our thanks to them for having us over."

Salma emulates Ziko by her vocal ad, with an Arabic language dressed in a fancy lace-trimmed French chapeau type accent. Our first tour takes off and we stop-by the village. Bakry and the crew help the tourists and Salma's mother off the felucca.

Landing on the village is like stepping back in time. Little huts made out of mud brick and colored in beautiful pastels, surrounded by palm groves. It could've been mistaken for a Spanish Villa if it isn't for the chickens and goats running around and the fact that it has no pool. In the village, baby crocodiles are the pets. I find Nubians are quite courteous and hospitable. Tourists watch in awe, and then walk-off exploring the village and taking pictures.

Salam's eyes catch a little seven-year old girl looking at the tourists navigating her village. Salma smiles, the little girl grins back and reaches for Salma's hand.
"What's your name?" the girl asks.
"Salma. What's yours?"
"Cena. What's that in your hand?"
"This is an iPod."
"What is it for?"
"Here…" Salma places her earphones on Cena. The girl jolts for a second. Her eyebrows run high and her smile grows wider.
"Oh, my god," she giggles.

We finish our first tour and return to the port. Passengers are waiting in lines. The departing travelers are raving about our program '*such a heart-warming experience*' they say. I take a glimpse at Captain Moustache and Captain Hook. They are dying of jealousy.

In the middle of our second tour, we hear loud sirens. "Clear the Way" sergeant Wahby instructs in a microphone. He is standing aboard a white police motorboat deliberately heading towards us. "I repeat, Clear the Way."

"Everyone calm down, stay put and remain seated," Bakry instructs firmly.

I move towards Captain Bakry... "How can I help?"

"We are now closer to the island than we are to the port. They won't give us a chance to return to the port. But the wind is pushing us towards the port. We need to steer against the wind to make it in-time to the island before they crash into us."

Bakry's action plan manages to anger the wind; it starts to pick up and to partner with the sergeant. Bakry holds on what he calls a "Tiller". It is a wooden handle attached to the rudder. He pushes the tiller to the left. The boat tends to turn right but then the wind opposes the turning. The boat swings; the crowd screams and Wahby blows in his evacuate horn; it sounds like one crazy orchestra.

"This isn't working" Bakry says, heavy sweat drops are covering his forehead and dripping from under his arms. "Ready About," he shouts and the crew takes different positions on the felucca. Bakry pushes the tiller harshly to the right.

"Are we going with the wind now? Are we heading to the port?" I ask.

"No, we are turning the felucca into the wind," Bakry decides.

"It sounds scary," Salma interjects.

"Trust me," Bakry affirms. Salma freezes for a minute then takes her seat.

Bakry's crew pulls in the sails. The sails drift towards the middle of the boat. The crew tightens the ropes. Bakry is still pushing the tiller. The felucca is jiggling hard. Salma's mother is screaming like some passengers. Salma tries to calm everyone down. The evacuate horn blows again.

"Move to the center," Bakry shouts, "Heads Down," he instructs his crew.

The boom swings very quickly across the boat. It feels as if we are caught in a Tornado when the midpoint of the felucca reaches what seems like the highest circle of the wind. Bakry dives underneath the boom with his maneuver, and then quickly moves to the new upwind side by constantly turning. We are no longer facing into the wind. We are far enough off. The evacuate horn blows one more time.

"Move to the high side," Bakry orders. "Oars," he commands. The crew distributes oars, one for each passenger. "Move Forward, Start Oaring," Bakry instructs. The crew guides the passengers. Everyone moves to the forward side of the felucca. The oars are dipped in the water and everyone rafts except for Salma's mother... "I can't do that". Salma glares at her mother and rafts as hard as she can with her oar.

Bakry pushes his tiller the other side while shouting... "Move Back, Keep oaring". The crew guides the passengers again and everyone moves to the backside of the felucca and the oaring continues in synchronization. The evacuate horn blows.

"Come About," Bakry commands and the crew starts filling the sails. I look on the right and I am amazed to see that we are lining up with the island. I shift my gaze and I see big shadow casted on our boat. "Move to the Right", I hear Bakry shouting. He steers the boat as fast as he can. Our boat tilts and turns on its side at the same second that Wahby's police motorboat zooms by and shoves the left side of our boat. The felucca rises up the ground before it blasts on the island, then everything darkens.

I am not sure how long it has passed before I become aware of my surroundings. All I know is that as I open my eyes, I see lots of faces looking at me.

"Saad, are you OK?" asks Salma. Her eyes wide open and her face pale white.

"I am good, I am good" I try to sit up, but as I try to lean on my left arm, I feel that it only qualifies to be a lettuce leaf. Enormous pain shoots through my head, "AWE" I hear myself almost screaming. I look at my arm; it's lying there, but not talking to my body anymore. Neither is my left foot.

"What happened?" I ask.

"The rudder landed on your left side. The rudder was still moving apparently when the felucca got thrown on the island, so it got your left side really bad," Bakry clarifies. Salma cries... "Oh, my god."

We hear the police boat returning back and Wahby walks steadily towards us.

"Look what you did," Salma shouts. "You almost killed him. Why did you have to do that? We were close to the island already."

Wahby smiles calmly, looks at me, and then navigates the crowd... "Security Measures, the waters needed to be cleared at this second. Maybe your helmsman is still in training."

"Captain Bakry did a great job," Salma defends.

"Captain? That's a nice title," Wahby mocks.

"OK, for all non-Egyptians, please come aboard our boat, we're taking you to your hotels. Time is of the essence. The waters need to be clear again in 30 minutes," Wahby announces. Passengers start moving towards his boat with the assistance of his men.

"What do you mean non-Egyptians?" Salma stands in front of Wahby.

"Our boat is designed for only 15 passengers. With you, your old lady, the injured driver, your Captain and the crew, we are talking 25. The passengers are currently 13. We have room for two more. Would you and your old lady like to hop on?"

"Yes, thank you sergeant," replies Salma's mother with a flattering smile.

"**NO**," Salma holds her mother back. "Take Saad instead, he needs to go to the hospital," Salma demands.

"Sorry, hospital is on the other side, totally off course. I'll call for an emergency helicopter though to come and pick him up. Last call, do you want to leave those rural people, whom you clearly don't belong to and join us on our safe comfortable boat?"

"No," Salma insists.

"Salma," her mother squeezes her arm.

"I am not leaving Saad," Salma decides.

"Fine, don't say I didn't ask," Wahby closes with a sleazy smile.

The boat leaves. No sign of any helicopter appears on the horizon for hours. Some villagers bring some water and food for me. Captain Bakry tries to help me sit up but I truly can't move an inch. The tea that I am offered, by the people here makes the pain a little bit tolerable, but not for long.

*'It is going to be OK '*حبيبي *– habiby' (my love), you are a tough boy; Mother raised you tough. What doesn't kill you makes you stronger, always remember that, '* – I can see my mother's face clearer than ever though, and I can feel my soul lighter than ever.

"This is all, my fault. I should have listened to Nadeem. He warned me and I just thought he was showing off. This is all, my fault," Salma cries.

"Oh, Nadeem, Yes, I have their cell phone numbers here, try and contact them," Salma's mother says.

"Look at him, he is sweating, bleeding and losing his consciousness. Saad, stay with us, Saad!" I die and lose sight of all of them.

Few hours later, a nudge on my chest brings me back to life. I see Nadeem's face. He pushes some pills down my throat.

"Swallow," he instructs and pours some water in my mouth, while his other hand is lifting my head and supporting my neck.

"Saad, I need you to work with me. I'll take you home."

"Is the helicopter here?"

"No, we'll swim"

"**SWIM??** Mr. Nadeem, I am half broken, how can I swim?"

Nadeem stands... "We need some wooden blades."

"Here, you'll find only wooden logs, but no blades," replies Bakry.

"Unless..." he pauses.

"What?" Nadeem asks.

"That's fine, it is broken anyway. You can use parts of my boat," Bakry says.

"Are you sure?"

"Yes"

"We'll compensate you, I promise," Nadeem says.

I fall in a brief coma and as I wake-up, I catch a glimpse of Nadeem snapping some blades from the felucca sleeping on its side. He snaps, breaks, assembles and erects. Bakry looks at his felucca been snatched into pieces. Sadness is building up in his eyes.

"Hey, Saad, this has been tough for you, but I need you to tolerate some more and work with me," Nadeem says. He lifts my arm and I scream "AWE", he places my arm carefully between two blades. Salma hands him a huge sticky tape, which he has brought with him. He starts rolling it around the blades. He does the same with my leg.

"Wouldn't the adhesive material dissolve in the river?" Salma asks.

"Eventually it will, but it is durable enough to take us to the other side."

Nadeem finishes wrapping me.

"I'll be back to take you and your mother."

"No, I'll stay with the crew, we came together, and we'll leave together."

Nadeem shakes his head in dismay. "Are you sure?"
"Absolutely," Salma's words contradict with the look on her mother's face.

"Oh, I envy you, broken thing," her mother's eyes tell me.

The Tomb Opens

CHAPTER THIRTEEN

The Savior – Seven Souls

The night pulls a blanket of darkness and hides us. My back is straightened on a wooden slab and both my left arm and leg are sandwiched between wooden blades. Nadeem ties a rope around my waist then extends a loose part before he ties it again around his waist. He is literally carrying me in this open summery coffin, and slowly sinks under the water like a crocodile. Funny thing is that Aswan used to have lots of crocodiles, thank god not anymore, although I saw some babies on the island. OK, I won't think about that now. I want to be as light as possible on Nadeem's back but I am not sure how.

*'Saad, focus '*حبيبي *– habiby' (my love), Take care, Saad, I am praying for you.'* – Oh, this isn't good. We were used to hear Ma's soft tone only when someone was dying. I must be really messed up.

It is very dark until we come closer to the old Cataract hotel that is beaming with light and music. Nadeem's head emerges and he whispers... "Listen, Saad, this is a very critical place, hang on to my side and we'll try to glide so slowly. We have to cause no bubbling, no waving, and no attention of any kind. Understood?"

We glide smoothly but Nadeem stops as we overhear Wahby's voice talking to someone on the deck in a hush-hush tone:

"I am positive Sir. They are conspiring a new form of revolutionary act. I took all measurements to keep their actions limited but they seem to have some external support because they are daring and won't back off. They try to earn the trust and love of the people here in order to pave the road and move them as puppets wherever way they want. And who knows, maybe they are starting here but will expand to Alexandria then Cairo. It's a threat Sir and they look trained. This is no less than a secret intelligence mission and apparently Nadeem Sabry has been planted in our internal force department for years so he has the inside information. They are after the current regime and I bet on it with my life."

"Listen, sergeant, we won't allow any despicable meaningless air bubble to disturb us. Some people think they know better but their ignorance drives them to their graves. We can't raise any formal allegations without proofs though. Do what you need to do and you have my full support. Don't give yourself the liberty to pull the trigger without consulting me, though. I need factual reports: pictures, discussions, actions, path routes, everything. There will always be a time, when the media needs to get some attraction and prove that they are working. Always wait for my green light. The operation needs to run professionally, clean and quiet. Understood?"

"Yes, Sir"

No matter how much I try, my wooden leg keeps coming up in a supreme desire to float. Unaware that I am not in a vertical position like he is, Nadeem glides and bumps into my wooden leg and the disturbed waves tell on us.

"Someone is here," Wahby gets alerted, as the water bubbles and the waves dance around Nadeem and I. Nadeem turns me over exposing my back-supporting wooden slab to the surface and submerging my body under it. He pulls me so vigorously that I feel that my broken arm and leg just fell back. I hear lots of footsteps, I see bright flashes reflected on the surface of the water, and I even hear some gunshots and the hovering sound of a helicopter. Could this be the helicopter coming to rescue me? But then I feel the urge to breath, my left side is numb, I wish I can express my pain, but everything starts to fade away, I hear no evil, I see no evil, and I speak no evil. I die once more. *'Saad!'* – Coming Ma.

"How are you doing Saad?" – It sounds like Dr. Rashad's voice, but echoing from afar. I push my heavy eyelids and open a slit of window to the external world. It looks so neat and white in here; maybe I made it to paradise. I don't see my mother's face though. Could it be that we aren't at the same eternal ending?

"Saad?" I hear again, and I try to open my eyes a little wider but I fail. I touch my left side. My left limbs are in a hard shell.

"Saad, can you hear me?"

"Yes," I reply, my eyes glue shut.

"We thank the lord," Dr. Rashad says. "Two months and you'll be back to normal. They say that it could have been worse if you hadn't had those wooden blades on".

I am still alive. *'You've got seven souls, like a cat, 'حبيبي – habiby' (my love),'* – Thanks Ma. I was worried about you.

It takes me a couple of hours to be able to slightly open my eyes. Bassim pushes the door and jogs happily in the room. Ziko follows him, holding a basket of fruits.

"I thought flowers are for girls. But the hospital prohibited cheese, meat, dairy and deserts. I was left with nothing but fruits and this large chewy loaf of bread that you can bite on, every time you feel a pain. By the way, the nurse outside can relieve any pain you're ever feeling," Ziko winks.

"How is Nadeem?" I ask, the fact that Nadeem isn't accompanying Bassim is quite alarming.

"Nadeem is fine, very mild hypothermia. He needs some rest. It was unusually cold last night and he swam with you for five hours before Ziko and the paramedics spotted them on the other side. They formed a chain of hands until they managed to get both of you out of the water," Dr. Rashad explains.

"Five hours? I passed away for five hours and he kept carrying me? Wow. He is such an iron-man."

"He said that he stopped to catch his breath numerously, sometimes by hanging on to one of the huge rocks resting in the Nile River and sometimes by hanging on to your wooden blades. You were happily sleeping while floating on your back. Oh, speaking of your blades, it turns out your leg isn't broken, they casted it because they needed it to remain still for a few weeks. But you should be out of here in a couple of days," Dr. Rashad says.

"Thank you all very much. What about Salma?"

"Salma and her mother are fine. She is in touch by SMS."

"Oh, so they are still on the island?"

"Yes"

In her white gown and tied-up hair-bun, the nurse that Ziko has recommended, helps me place buttocks in a wheel chair and guides me to Nadeem's room as the proud sun falls a bit towards the west.

"Thanks, appreciate it," A smile floats on Nadeem's face as he hangs up the phone.

"He is coming," Nadeem declares. Dr. Rashad nods from the corner of the room.

"Who?" I ask. Wahby answers my question by walking in.

"Sergeant Wahby, very nice of you to come and check on me," Nadeem says.

"I am just doing my job," he smiles. "I see Saad is back. Did you fly back Pal? I guess not. I hear the crocodiles took a bite of your leg," he laughs.

"So former lieutenant Sabry, I am afraid you are in violation of the national and internal security laws. You created and practiced a security breach by making your way to and from the island. I am sure you know something like this can't go un-noticed and it is certainly punishable."

Nadeem smiles widely. He raises his voice and looks behind Wahby: "Chief Inspector, Omar Salah, welcome."

Wahby's eye-pupils roll in his skull for few seconds before his brain interprets Nadeem's words. He turns and is faced by the Chief inspector.

"Thanks lieutenant Sabry," Chief Omar walks steadily in the room; his voice deep and gruff. He sits on the chair next to Nadeem's bed.

"As per our phone call, I understand your concern about your second cousin Salma and I assure you that we'll bring her back safely," says Chief Salah.

"Thanks Chief Salah, I am concerned about an action that took place without any announced regulation and ran against the basic safety human rights on a felucca that carried thirteen tourists. I know they were escorted later but imagine the headlines on the global news describing how a police motorboat attacked a tourists' felucca in Egypt, that's why I contacted you.

Sergeant Wahby was alerting my attention right now about how I violated the un-announced regulations by bringing Saad to the hospital after being severely injured as a result of the brutal 'Clear the Way' method that was used. Picture Saad's photo on the news on CNN or BBC or CBC; think about the ramifications."

"You did the right think lieutenant Sabry, it isn't the first time we work together and you know I trust your judgment." Chief Salah glares at Wahby.

"As per our phone conversation, I am asking about the legitimate procedure to file a complaint against the police forces that conducted the felucca breakage action; run investigations and see fair consequential actions take place. See, what I am asking for, is currently being asked by some of the tourists, who witnessed and lived the circumstances, plus my second cousin Salma and her mother have double nationality and they are suing."

Wahby's face turns turmeric yellow. His eyes open and shut in an annoying eye blinking tic.

"Chief Salah, do you see that I have a valid concern here?"

"You certainly have a valid point. But this is Aswan not Cairo or Alexandria. We don't have such luxury of having a complaint system with a group of investigators, analytics and judges; and let's forget this is Egypt, not America. But we are willing to rectify any physical or psychological damage that may have occurred."

"I understand that perfectly well, Chief Salah, and I know that such news can hurt the reputation of the police existence here in Aswan and can be an alarming statement on the reports of all who are involved." Chief Salah throws another glare at sergeant Wahby.

"The problem, chief, lies in the evidence that is still bearing and alive. See, the felucca is a total wreck. My cousin, her mother and the crew are still stranded on the island."

"Bakry's felucca will be fixed and if it is totally damaged, it will be replaced for him. Your cousin and the crew will be taken aboard a fine police motorboat and returned back to the port. Sergeant Wahby, these are my orders, make sure they are executed before the night falls."

"Yes, Sir"

"See, Chief Salah, it's very rare to find a police man in your rank who can be open-minded, admitting lack of communication in some circumstances and is willing to own problems and fix them."

"Thank you, lieutenant Sabry for bringing this matter to my attention. We are trying to be good role models for the youngsters and do our job to the best of our ability."

"As you probably know, Chief, I left the force. I am now in the process of starting my own private business, a 'Threat Assessment Organization'."

Sergeant Wahby's eyes stop twitching and form a couple of squinted lines. Chief Salah leans forward; his ear lobs pop outside, and the tips of his right hand fingers touch the tips of his left hand fingers forming a ball.

"Is it like a private detective type of organization?"

"No, it is an organization that analyzes the given circumstances or maybe events like the summit but before they take place. Based on pre-defined suspicious factors and similar events and circumstances around the world, it then draws a chart of the potential threats in a certain area and highlights those threats to the authorities, plus drafting an action plan and an accountability matrix."

"Interesting, what a BRILLIANT idea, lieutenant Sabry. I sure would like to hear more about this. We can benefit a lot from such initiative. Sergeant Wahby, are you aware of any legitimate threats that are being overlooked or not thoroughly studied? We can certainly start exploring lieutenant Sabry's idea."

"I am willing to share my expertise and provide guidance to your department at any time Chief," Nadeem offers. "I have a curriculum in mind that will transform the image of the police force on the streets in Aswan. It is a total mind-shift strategy."

"That's very noble of you lieutenant Sabry to quit your job, of supporting civilians' safety and switch gears to support your fellow peers. I assure you that in Aswan, our department takes every action to make sure tourists are comfortable and every precaution to make sure that their stay is safe. I do have a question though. Will your organization be a private independent contractor or is it tied with the government and the national security?" Wahby asks.

All eyes shift to Nadeem but his answer doesn't come fast enough.

"The reason being, if it is a private independent organization, then all sorts of customers may knock on the door; each has their own agenda, interest, and one can only imagine the massive amount of conflict that can arise.

On the other hand, if it is legalized and sponsored by the government and the national security department, there can be a duplicate of effort plus some conflict of interest." Wahby elaborates.

"I am still designing my business plan. But great question, Sergeant."

Chief Salah's smile fades, his gaze freezes, his mind sinks in thoughts. He nods then stands-up; extends his hand to Nadeem.

"Good luck on your private business. Let's stay in touch, so I can be up to date with your progress."

I watch them leave the hospital from Nadeem's room window.

"This sergeant is a quick-witted fellow. He killed your idea in its womb and blurred your heroic image that you were busy painting for the Chief. I believe the Chief is no more a card for you, Nadeem, but you've certainly earned yourself a fierce enemy," Dr. Rashad concludes. Nadeem remains silent.

The Tomb Opens

CHAPTER FOURTEEN

Cats Fight

Dr. Rashad takes my seat and drives the cab. "Have you seen that boy crossing the street suddenly unalarmed that a car is passing?" He presses harshly on the brakes…

"The mother just turned her head, yelled at the chain of kids she drags behind her back, and moved on as if nothing happened. Lack of education is eating every bit of you, Egypt." He steps on the gas…

"How can someone be listening to music this loud? I am turning deaf just by being in the car next to his."

"This guy in the red car is changing lanes extensively. He must be drunk or on drugs."

"Oh, for god's sakes, he is eating in a plate with utensils while driving."

Dr. Rashad is quite an observant and his mind exaggerates what his eyes spot on the fly. I bet too much education leads to that.

"This woman is tailgating me on a one way street, I speed up but she still follows, I swear to god if she rams into my car, I mean your cab, I'll…"

"Maybe the guy in the red car isn't on drugs after all and he is just running away from that woman tailgating you. I say we park on the side and let them handle their issues," Ziko humors.

"Well, if it weren't for Mr. Funny," Dr. Rashad replies in dismay.

We reach our apartment physically safe but mentally damaged. I swear to god if I had Dr. Rashad's gloomy view of the world, I would have quit this job and worked in a laundry place. I think I am going to stick to walking, or limping to be more accurate, until I can drive again. I make myself an inky dark cup of tea in hopes to scare the headache away. The doorbell rings. The ladies arrive.

"Oh, my god Saad, look at all the casts. I am very sorry. How are you feeling?" asks the beauty. She looks more like Cinderella now, before the fairy godmother.

"All better, thanks"

The ladies take turns showering. Salma sits on the sofa in the living room. She has no make-up on and is wearing a plain white T-shirt that looks a couple of sizes bigger than her fit and a pair of beige pants. It is as if she has been bleached. Her mother emerges from her room hugging a fur coat.

"Oh, I so missed you," she talks to the coat.

"Excuse me?" Salma ridicules.

"What?"

"You missed FUR!! We are out on an island, sharing shelters with strange people; spending long hours in the dark uncertain on what will come next; meeting individuals who have way less than the basic needs of living, yet generous enough to share their bites of food with us; surrounded by kids who are ill, sick, partially naked, uneducated yet smile and play as if offering the world unconditional friendliness, children who hug us genuinely when we show them some kindness, and you miss your precious FUR? Why did you even bring it, it is Aswan for gods sakes, meaning very hot?"

"Salma, what got into you?"

"Why did you even come, mom?" Salma asks in disappointment.

"For you and yes, I miss my FUR. I miss my life style. It is not my fault that some people are less fortunate than I am. It isn't even my responsibility to make the world better for them. It's the government role and I give charity. I came here because nana told me that you immigrated. You didn't have the courtesy to say goodbye to your own mother. Besides, we both know that you can never risk losing the life style that you grew accustomed to. You are criticizing me, young lady. We are two faces of the same coin cut". Salma's mother takes her coat and heads to the bedroom, but then stops at the doorway and turns…

"I tolerated all the terrible things those past two days just so you'd understand what you are getting yourself into; and I hope you learned your lesson. People were using either Nile water directly or their sewage water to clean themselves, cook food and water their crops. Is this the kind of life that you chose for yourself?"

"They didn't choose to live that humble either."

"Listen I am leaving this evening, whether you are coming with me or not". Salma's mother slams the bedroom door shut.

"I am a big girl and I have to break free – I have to break free." Salma murmurs.

The Tomb Opens

CHAPTER FIFTEEN

Second Blow

Salma drifts off on the sofa. Dr. Rashad passes by and casually without looking he throws a light blanket on her. Nadeem spends long time on his laptop, on his phone, going out and coming in. Ziko has been at the museum all day.

I catch Dr. Rashad playing with Bassim 'hide and seek'. At a certain point, he tries to teach the kid how to play chess, but Bassim uses all the pieces in his newly invented game 'Shoot the Target', where he aims at Dr. Rashad's eyeglasses… "Illiterate kid, just like his father".

Five o'clock, Salma's mother leaves. The hug and cheek-kiss that they share are too cold for a couple of hot ladies. My mother would kiss five times in a row, all vocally clear and she would compress the lungs of the person she is hugging. I guess she was a very affectionate woman. Salma and I decide to take a walk to check on Ziko.

Ziko is standing on the side while a Nubian youth is performing his show.

"Hey Ziko, what's going on?" Salma asks.

"A German group showed-up. Hamada who has been watching my show, offered to perform for them. He is doing an amazing job. Osman recruited two more craftsmen to help with his collection. He is making very good sales. You are back. How are you?"

"I am a bit shaken, but I'll be better. Mother left. Bakry got a new felucca and he is really happy about it."

The crowd interacts well with Hamada's animated demonstration.

"Looks like you've been cloned, Ziko," Salma muses.

"Come on, was I ever that good?" Ziko jokes.

I don't know if it is just me – but Ziko and Salma seem a little carried away to me. They are excited about others' success and happiness more than they are excited about their assignments. I am no expert, here, but shouldn't Ziko be at different locations instead of watching Hamada? Shouldn't Salma start her sense-of-belonging homework already? Something has gotten into those two.

'Saad, 'حبيبي – habiby' (my love), you care too much for people. Cut it out.' Always correcting my course, Ma. God, I can't make an observation without getting the commentator's line.

Back at home, we, each head to their bedroom feeling quite content. The events of the day promise us a good night sleep. I set my crutches aside and carefully slide myself under the nice cold covers. I don't quite get that 'good' and 'peace' aren't included in the contract.

The eyelids that have closed peacefully for the night are pulled wide open and the sweat that has smoothed our hair on our pillows, turns into hardening gel as we wake-up in the morning at the sound of Ziko yelling. We all open our rooms' doors and we all look as if we just got electrocuted. Ziko is furiously talking to Nadeem in the hallway.

"You got to do something."

"I'll get dressed and head to the station," Nadeem says, sluggish from sleep and hardly opening just one eye.

"What's going on?" Salma asks.

"They arrested Osman for possession of an original Nefertari head."

The news hit us hard. We freeze for a couple of minutes.
"And so it begins…" Dr. Rashad notes.
"You people thought the felucca attack was the real deal. This Wahby guy waited, planned and took his shot. I bet it isn't going to be just this, we are up against a series of shots."

"With all due respect Dr. Rashad, Osman already showed interest in this mischievous path. Maybe Wahby doesn't have anything to do with this. Are you certain, Ziko, that Osman didn't steal the monument?" Salma asks.
Ziko's eyes shoot fury.

"He did not do it," he affirms, talking slowly through his clenched teeth. Then he joins Nadeem down the stairs.

"He can't be that sure. But …whatever. What do you say, Saad, we head off to the port and see how things are with Bakry? I'll buy you breakfast." Salma offers.

"Are you planning on going on another tour?" I ask.

"Will you join me if I do?" she asks me back.

"Sure, why not?"

"Aren't you scared, we may get attacked again?"

"I survived the first one. God helps those who help themselves. By going-on with my life, I am helping myself. I am a cab driver. I earn my living using: my two arms, hands and legs. Crying in the corner won't heal my pain, living through it as if it didn't happen will."

'Well said, 'حبيبي – habiby' (my love), Mama raised you well. You know this didn't come from your father. ' – I am forever grateful mom.

"Ok, Saad, I'll be ready in 30 minutes."

Salma drives the cab. She pulls her stylish beret to cover her forehead. She looks left and right as if checking if anyone can see her. She seems not that thrilled at the experience of driving a cab. She actually looks rather embarrassed. I understand. She used to be a princess. But somehow I am feeling offended. No, I am not. Yes, I am.

Salma drives for 20 minutes before her eyes catches my face in the rear mirror. Because of how big my leg and arm are in the casts, I am now taking the passenger seat in the back. The front seat hurts me when whoever drives keeps speeding and braking.

"Saad, are you feeling OK?"

"I am a cab driver Miss Salma, and I am not ashamed of it. But I understand. It's OK. I am cool."

Salma's face turns plum red. She blinks more as she looks down at the driving wheel then back at me in the mirror.

"I am sorry, Saad." Salma pushes the beret off her forehead a bit, and then looks at me. I smile. She does this several times. I keep on smiling. Then she pulls the beret off her head completely and throws it on the seat next to her.

"Saad, could you please be my navigator and guide the way to the port?"

"Certainly," I say proudly.

Our visit to the port lasts only few minutes, after which we rush to the police station to catch-up with Nadeem and Ziko. Salma assists me out the cab and in the station.

"So, you are here for Osman?" Wahby mocks.

"What? Is he your second cousin too?" He adds sarcastically.

"I am his lawyer and I hold you accountable if he suffers any physical abuse during the interrogation," Nadeem answers firmly.

"He is a thief and a traitor to his country," Wahby accuses.

"We'll meet at court then," Nadeem ends.

Salma whispers our findings at the port to Nadeem.

"Sergeant Wahby, I am representing both Osman and Bakry at court, and again, I'll be careful of any torture if I were you," Nadeem threatens.

"What did Bakry do?" Ziko asks in shock.

"He was planning a terrorist attack and we caught arms and weapons in his possession," Wahby provokes confidently.

"You are fighting for a lost cause, my friend," he tells Nadeem demonstrating a yellow smile.

"See you at court, sergeant," Nadeem turns and leaves the station. Ziko follows. Wahby exhales a sarcastic smile and draws a daring look that scares both Salma and I out of his office.

If I had my full gear of arms and legs, I would have been stepping on the gas back to Cairo by now. This isn't going to be pretty.

The Tomb Opens

CHAPTER SIXTEEN

Salma

On the balcony, my eyes catch a glimpse of the moon and I find myself mumbling some Shakespearean words that I cut off a magazine in the Canadian embassy quite some time ago…

"When I do count the clock that tells the time, and see the brave day sunk in hideous night; …"

'You're kidding, right?' – Oh, hello mom, long time since you last visited. But it's true though, with my broken parts, I count the minutes wishing for them to run quicker, and indeed today was a brave day with Nadeem defending Osman and Bakry, and with Salma coming out of her hide behind the beret.

'You still think of yourself as the 'Poet Lost Behind the Wheel' don't you?' – I shake my mother's image off my head and I look at the clock that reads 10:00 at night.

"Team Meeting," Dr. Rashad announces. We all gather in the living room.

"Salma, you haven't stopped crying since you came home. We are worried about you," Dr. Rashad says.

"Home? I was raised in Dubai where my father worked as a doctor. He was a well-respected doctor and everyone loved him. We lived in a very high-standard community; all were diplomats from around the world. 'Classy' was the one thing that my mother strove to be categorized under. 'Impress' was where she devoted her efforts.

My mother allowed me nothing but protocol. I was under a nanny's supervision all day long. I grew-up resentful of my parents because they were always busy, my father with his patients and career and my mother with her friends, galleries and shopping. I felt so distant from them. But every now and then my father would take a couple of days off and shower me with love and care. I wished for him to be more involved with my life though, to be more aware of my feelings but he didn't have the time for it.

My mother painted our home with her perception, thoughts and principles. Show-off and being materialistic weren't my dad's qualities. He didn't follow her but he also didn't stop her. He passed away when I was fifteen. I grew-up to be no different from my mom. I too am hypnotized by the 'Classy' illusion and 'Impress' remains my target.

But the couple of days we spent out there with nothing to cover our cold backs at night, and with wide-open eyes lest unexpected danger comes our way, helped me realize that I am not my mother. I value safety over luxury. I learned that a humble person is the person who helps you then leaves before you get to thank him or know his name, because he simply isn't awaiting any recognition. People helped us, hosted us, and shared their tiny bites of food with us, with absolutely nothing in return – just pure unconditional kindness. Something I never learned to offer or appreciate or even expect.

To watch the cops today handcuffing Bakry and shoving his head inside their jeep was so harsh for me on so many levels.

Deep down I wish my dad was like Bakry. Bakry takes pride in who he is, and he is a real ***CAPTAIN*** capable of saving his own crew and the people who entrusted him with their lives. He can see the land clear in front of him even through heavy clouds, blinding fog, or gloomy sky. He is harsh and rugged, like any virgin solid gem.

I am sorry for being so emotional. Bakry's first encounter with me was like a fatherly scolding, needed for the betterment of a good child.

Today, thirteen years later, I felt like I lost my father yet again." Salma sobs. Bassim gives her the tissue box. She blows her red nose and engages in what seems like endless crying. Through her tears, she continues.

"My mission is to promote sense of belonging. Me? Even nana, whom I truly love, I wasn't able to feel that I belong to her home. All my life, I felt like a lucky orphan; one whom people fed, dressed and entertained, but never did the walls of any of the places I inhibited formed a home for me, or constructed any sense of belonging; that's why I wanted to immigrate. I am simply leaving nothing behind; I belong to no-one and no-where. How on earth can I inspire a feeling in others if I don't personally have it?"

"Salma, are you crying because of what happened to Bakry or because of struggling in your mission?" Dr. Rashad asks. Salma doesn't answer for a couple of minutes.

"If I hadn't been on the island for a couple of days, subject to all sorts of abandonment, I know I would have turned a deaf ear to Bakry and convinced myself that it is his destiny. I know I would have visited his family, gave them some money and made my conscious content with it. But today, I can't, I just can't. Today, I am leaving no stone unturned to prove Bakry innocent. I know he is."

"Nadeem, what's your take on this? Fabricated or Coincidence?"

"Fabricated, absolutely. It's the common ear-pinching strategy, no doubt about it. Osman started to attract more like-minded candidates. It meant Ziko's plan was going well. Bakry's cooperation with Salma caused him damage that got rectified by a brand-new felucca. Next thing you know it, other felucca captains will emulate his style. It meant Salma's plan was going well. Wahby is suspicious and he believes that the more people we gather around us, the more likely we can lead a change, which in his mind can lead to a revolution or any disorder of any kind.

Arresting Osman and Bakry is targeted towards driving people away plus teaching those two a sour lesson. It doesn't mean we are off the hook, Wahby is just tying our hands before he strikes his shot at us."

"Beautiful," Dr. Rashad comments in admiration.

"Well sure, this twisted plot is **MUSIC** to your ears, but the people selling merchandise to earn their living, up-beat songs on the radio that keep people energetic despite the poverty and corruption, and kids running down the streets trusting the world to protect them, are all ugly and noisy. You have the weirdest taste in life, Papa," Ziko mocks sourly.

Dr. Rashad stands…"OK, listen up people. Proving Osman and Bakry innocent is our golden visa to Canada. But in order to get Osman and Bakry released, we need to work together as a team. Yes, you've got your own problems, and indeed you are all somehow troubled, but I am left with no choice but to hope that you still have a bit of strength engraved somewhere inside you. Working solo will render us an easy prey for Wahby to take us down one after the other. Are you on?"

They pause and look at each other.

"I am," Ziko stands and extends his arm with an open palm. Nadeem stands, and puts his hand on top of Ziko's. Salma puts her hand on top of Nadeem's. Dr. Rashad puts one hand under Ziko's and the other on top of Salma's.

"We are on," Dr. Rashad affirms.

Cool, the individuals who few weeks ago have embarked on a journey of uncertainty in my cab, criticizing and hating each other, are now forming a team coached by Dr. Rashad. Now, this is an interesting turn of events.

The Tomb Opens

CHAPTER SEVENTEEN

The Court

Nadeem's night-light has witnessed him sewing the darkness of the night to the brightness of the day. He restudies criminal law from a defendant perspective. He makes numerous calls. He informally interrogates people at the scene where Osman and Bakry have been arrested. He reads and examines the police reports.

"Osman's case is being assigned an archaeology and antiquities specialist. It is likely though that the Nefertari-head piece, found at Osman's place, is actually original. Wahby won't risk his credibility, building his case on a fake piece," Nadeem explains.

"Do we know the name of this specialist?" Dr. Rashad asks.

"Salem Mansur,"

"Oh, I went to school with that guy," Dr. Rashad announces.

"So?" Nadeem wonders.

"When is the hearing scheduled to take place?" Ziko asks.

"Monday. It is a national security issue. Cases like this take highest priority and get expedited."

"How long ago have you seen Salem Mansur, papa, Are you, by any chance, still in touch with him?" Ziko asks Dr. Rashad.

"Bribing the guy wouldn't help, if anything it will get Osman prosecuted," Nadeem objects firmly.

"Oh, we'll never do that," Ziko affirms, his eyes betraying his words.

"What about Bakry?" Salma asks.

"Bakry's case has some gaps in it that I can use."

"When is the hearing?"

"Also Monday"

Their gaze drop and their thoughts are set astray. The conversation dies between them.

Monday marathons over our heels and ignites our anxiousness. They call at Osman's case first. Osman looks fatter on the chest than before.

"Are you OK?" Nadeem asks.

"A couple of broken ribs," he answers.

"Session in order," it is announced. The plaintiff's attorney challenging Nadeem introduces himself as "Mouneer Shaker".

The session starts. Shaker talks big about the national security and the monuments that are being stolen and the betrayal of Egypt at the hands of people like Osman. He goes on and on working on boiling the blood in the jury's veins then he asks for the prosecution that people like Osman deserves.

It is Nadeem's turn. He calls upon the witnesses who all admit that Osman has always been a trust-worthy fellow and quite an artistic craftsman. They say that due to his fine work, he has been given the name: "***Imhotep the replicator***". Nadeem then calls the archaeology and antiquities specialist.

"In Mr. Salem Mansur's absence, I am Ibrahim Khufu, his assigned delegate," a voice echoes from the back of the courtroom.

A sturdy broad-shouldered handsome dirty-blond guy in a thick suit approaches the bench. He has a shaved beard and a dimple at the bottom of his boney chin. His tongue doesn't like to pronounce the letter "R", it sounds blurred and with a repeated effect "RRR". He has one broken tooth in the front that makes the "S" letter slip into a "TH".

"Your honor, submitted as exhibit one are: Mr. Khufu's credentials, his reference letters, the delegation letter from Salem Mansur who couldn't be here today due to health issues, along with his letter of apology, the tests that Mr. Khufu conducted on the antique in question, the reason he conducted such tests, the analysis that he did and the outcome of the analysis," Nadeem presents.

"Mr. Khufu, please step-up and come for the oath."

He does; then he answers all sorts of questions about himself and where and how he has been assigned the case. Everyone including the jury is asked if they accept him as a subject matter expert. He gets accepted. He is asked to share the results.

"Your honorrr, the antique in queTHtion *(question)* iTH *(is)* a rrreplica."

The crowd roars, Osman smiles, Wahby glares, "Yes": Salma cheers.

"It iTH *(is)* a verrry fine pieTHe *(piece)*, well-crrrafted. THome *(some)* of its parrrtTH *(parts)* arrre made of rrreal gold, which iTH *(is)* why it can be mistaken for a rrreal pieTHe *(piece)*. PluTH *(plus)* the colorrrTH *(colors)* are perrrmanent, rrrather opaque and lack the gloTHy *(glossy)* THurrrface *(surface)*, which again makeTH *(makes)* it a good rrreTHemblanTHe *(resemblance)* to an orrriginal pieTHe *(piece)*. It iTH *(is)* a job well done, but it iTHn't *(isn't)* an orrriginal. ThiTH *(this)* concludeTH *(concludes)* my rrreport, your honorrr and I stand by my findings."

Oh, dear god, I feel that every "RRR" has run a drill in my head and every "TH" has flushed the extra "R"s. My eyeballs are running all over the place inside my eye-socket. I gather myself and try to catch-up.

The plaintiff's attorney, Shaker, showers Khufu with tons of questions and at times accuses him indirectly of being incompetent or even a frailer and attacks his credibility. Nadeem catches Shaker's comments and asks for the support of the judge and the jury.

"Your honor, submitted as exhibit two is: a couple of certified reports from two other archaeology and antiquities specialists, confirming Mr. Khufu's analysis. Both specialists are present in the courtroom, ready to take the stand and give their oaths," Nadeem adds.

The plaintiff's attorney, Shaker, calls the specialists, interrogates them until the words abandon his questions leaving a big blank question mark on his face. The jury and judge decide that Osman is innocent and the charges get dropped.

"This isn't over," Wahby shots a glare at Nadeem and mumbles.

We are off for the break and we reconvene in one hour. Bakry enters the room, bruises coloring his face, his eyes are swollen shut, he looks at the world through a narrow squint, and he is quite limping. The session starts; Shaker delivers another speech to condemn the terrorist attacks and the innocent souls that get killed everyday at the hands of people like Bakry who possess a dead conscience. He supports his speech with vivid examples that torment the audience's hearts. Then he attacks Bakry and asks for the greatest prosecution. Nadeem calls upon six witnesses before he carries on with his defending speech.

"Your honor, this felucca has been given to Bakry the night before his arrest. He signed the ownership agreement but according to the witnesses and his crew he didn't get the chance to examine it."

"Objection, your honor, this is a lame argument," Shaker counterattacks.

"Proceed, counsel Sabry…"

"The arms and weapons found have the making and serial numbers that match some of the arms and weapons that were captured and confiscated in Rafah five months ago, during the arrest of three terrorists. I hereby submit the report filed in Rafah, as well as the report that lists the arms and weapons found on the felucca, as exhibit number one. "

The crowd roars. Wahby falls dead pale.

"Objection, your honor," Shaker interjects.

"Not quite lame now, is it?" Nadeem teases Shaker.

The judge calls for a break. After briefly consulting with Wahby, Shaker asks to proceed with the case confidentially in a closed set, but the judge decides it is too late.

Back in the courtroom, Nadeem proceeds harshly…
"How did the weapons in Rafah leave the possession of the internal forces and end-up in my client's felucca? Again, the internal forces gave this felucca to my client the night before his arrest. This is a planned and intended conviction and I hereby ask to drop the charges filed against my client and to hold the officials responsible for this plot, accountable."

"Counsel Shaker, any comments?"

"We weren't notified of the evidence in exhibit number one. An authorized subject matter expert needs to compare the Rafah list and the Aswan list and provide the court with a certified report. The submitted report is based on the attorney's eye-comparison and we can't possibly determine if the defendant is punishable or not based on a report pulled together manually by the defendant's attorney. I do request postponing the case."

"Case postponed to next Monday, session adjourned".
Bakry remains in custody.

"This isn't over," Nadeem teases Wahby out loud.

The Tomb Opens

CHAPTER EIGHTEEN

Victory

Back at home, I feel proud of myself. I can fill, brew, sip and pour five nice hot cups of tea in one minute, with one hand. I am definitely mastering this disablement thing.

"I don't get it, you already warned him not to physically hurt them, and yet they are both brutally beaten. We have to sue him, he didn't cooperate," Salma fumes.

"This isn't brutality. This is just one hour of beating. Wahby ordered his men to stop the interrogating torture after my warning, so technically he cooperated," Nadeem clarifies.

"One hour? A couple of broken ribs, limping and facial deformation, in just one hour? This is bullying and oppression," Salma says in devastation.

"Welcome to the reality of our law enforcement representatives / human-rights violators / empowered criminals / police officers of our beloved nation, Egypt," Ziko mocks.

"No offence buddy," He pats Nadeem's back lightly; then he gets up, takes both his teacup and Dr. Rashad's and head towards the balcony to join Dr. Rashad's 6:00 pm reflection time.

Dr. Rashad has noted so many times never to get interrupted during his half-an-hour daily reflection time but this never seems to stop Ziko from barging right in.

"Unbelievable. What else do you people do and how can you possibly sleep at night knowing that you exerted your power on others? What are the qualities needed in a police officer then? A sadistic nature?"

"Listen," Nadeem sighs.

"No, seriously, is that what you people are being taught at police academy? To push people's buttons and drive them to the edge using torture? You aren't seeking to construct or guide any improvement in the mind-set of law-offenders then; you are seeking elimination, exactly like we crush bugs. How can you people live with yourselves after that? Do you feel proud? Is your ego being fed big time by abusing others?"

"Salma," Nadeem tries to talk but Salma isn't looking for any answers. It is like she has been harshly nudged awake on an ugly reality. I don't see an end to this one-sided conversation so I drag my casted leg to the closest open door, the balcony. Sorry Dr. Rashad, I have no other choice.

***"No, seriously Ziko, you are quite talented**. I won't ask about the hair or the way of talking but how did you temporarily shed the fat and drop few sizes down?"*

"Under the suit, was a diving suit that magically tucks in excessive wobbly fat," Ziko answers.

"You are a genius. The Chin, how on earth did you hide your double chin? Did you tuck it in too?" Dr. Rashad asks in curiosity. Ziko exhales a sarcastic smile.

"It is a new treatment. The procedure is quite similar to having a tattoo. It is administered through a series of 40 to 70 mini-injections and works by dissolving small volumes of fat cells. The treatment is under study here in Egypt. I volunteered last week. I overdosed, hence the noticeable chin-dimple. But I won't complete the series of injections, I love my Santa Clause chin," Ziko replies.

"Impressive, really impressive," Dr. Rashad praises Ziko.

"Well, without your help papa, Mr. Mansur would have been in charge and Khufu wouldn't have been born," Ziko humors.

"Mansur is a health-freak, has always been. He took a couple of doses of the Asian spices that I once tried on Nadeem. His body responded better than Nadeem though but he is more paranoid. The first signs of diarrhea scared the hell out of him. He is now writing his will and is undergoing blood, urine and stool tests. With diarrhea, it wasn't hard to introduce him to Khufu and have him become his entrusted assistant then delegatee."

"See, who knew that diarrhea, can have such a rapid and effective effect?" Ziko mocks.

"Actually, studies show that emotional distress is associated with diarrhea. The patient feels: 1) I don't control the diarrhea, the diarrhea controls me; 2) I feel ashamed, dirty, and tainted; and 3) I fear what the diarrhea is doing to me and what it means. Naturally, not all people respond this way, Nadeem didn't but the older you get, the more vulnerable you become."

"Dr. Rashad, I am the one who is really impressed now. I know I always mocked your researches. But today I realized that I undervalued something that can possibly save people's lives, or in this case, can possibly harm people. So tell me something, papa, do you often do such experiments on people? And how does your conscious feel about that?"

"I sometimes do, but for the sake of science, not to intentionally hurt anyone, and I tell participants in advance and have them sign consents. This is the first time I do it to teach Nadeem a lesson and to help Osman's case. Ethically I am torn between feeling guilty and proud. Now, back to our case, what if they track the other two specialists down and re-open the case?"

"Dr. Rashad, please give me some credit here, will you? The antique piece that the two specialists examined, which is currently at the court custody is not an original."

"So, what happened to the original piece that was put in Osman's possession?"

"Oh, that one?"

"Yes, that one."

"Somehow it got replaced by the fake one when Mansur was putting Khufu in charge."

"You had the guts to replace it, right under the nose of the police officers?" Dr. Rashad asks in amazement.

"Oh, Stop, papa, you're making me feel prouder than I already am," Ziko looks down in a humble act, lifts his injected chin up and winks.

"They can re-open the case as many times as they want, the original piece evaporated; unless they want to give me another original piece for free."

"Won't they know it by looking at the fake one?"

"Actually the fake one is extremely good. It is one of Osman's unique antiques. His fiancée dumped him because he melted his gold engagement ring in crafting this piece. She was one of the witnesses on the case."

"Beautiful"

"What is beautiful? I have been listening to nothing but ugly attacks and descriptions since we came back from court," Nadeem interposes as he steps on the balcony. Ziko doesn't answer. He looks at Dr. Rashad.

"Tell us, Nadeem, how did you know that the making and serial numbers of the weapons and arms matched the ones confiscated in Rafah, or was that a trick?"

"Not a trick. You can't win by trickery. This is a fact. See, I happened to work on the Rafah case before I left the force. I wasn't sure of the making and serial numbers until I did some phone calls and got the report – a smudged copy, so my friends over there don't get in trouble. It was pure luck for Bakry and terrible luck for Wahby. That's all."

"Well I guess we need some research capabilities, hard work, some good luck and a bit of trickery to be able to live in Egypt. This is just too sad. But hey, today is our victory day and we have to celebrate," Dr. Rashad comments. "Where is Salma?"

"She is experiencing a post reality-check trauma," Nadeem replies.

"What's with your chin, Ziko, you seem to be itching it quite a bit?" Nadeem asks.

"It's a side-effect."

"What?"

"Oh, I mean, I am letting my beard grow and itching usually happens, so I am calling it a side-effect."

"I see"

"Mama"

Dr. Rashad leans closer to Ziko, as Nadeem checks Bassim's finger, which he complains, has a cut. "Are you seriously growing your beard?"

"I have to, till I regain my charming chin back."

"Unbelievable!" we hear Salma shouting in aggravation.

The Tomb Opens

CHAPTER NINETEEN

Ashamed or Proud?

We pant as we try to catch-up with the events that swirl rapidly over the course of a week. Osman's trial doesn't get re-opened. His reputation skyrockets because of the trial and fame builds around his antiques that are comparable to original ancient handcrafted pieces. His booth expands; he hires six craftsmen and starts teaching them. The line-up of buyers forms a zigzag shape to accommodate the rise in demand.

"What you perceive as the worst thing that ever happened to you, may turn out to be the best thing that ever happened to you," Osman tells Ziko excitedly.

"Always! You freak when you see the genie but as life unfolds its wicked plan for you, you become grateful you've found Aladdin's lamp and the genie saves your life," Ziko replies. They share a light-hearted laugh.

"Listen, I don't know how to thank you and Mr. Nadeem. You know, I got amazing offers after the trial, some of them with unbelievable compensation if I agree to leave Egypt and work abroad. You won't believe the figures and numbers, it's mind-blowing," Osman says.

"Awesome! Wow, now you're going to be a celebrity and I'll brag that one time we shared a sandwich and a can of coke. So which offer did you pick?"

"Oh, I declined the long-term travelling idea. I did my best work here. Bit by bit, I'll expand and add sophisticated tools and technological enablers. I will travel to promote my stuff, but I won't leave permanently."

"Oh come on, Osman, why not? This is a big break for you," Ziko asks in disbelief.

"Where else will I find people like you and Mr. Nadeem? You, Ziko, genuinely helped me believe in my talent and myself. This piece that brought me fame was on the top of my list to sell, but you convinced me to hold-on to it and use it as my brand. Mr. Nadeem didn't think twice before jumping in to be my defence attorney. And what did I offer you in return, what were you expecting? Nothing. This brother-like chivalry is like an antique nowadays, forever valued but impossible to replicate. But since I am the "***Imhotep the replicator***", I will stay to pass on what you, two, gave me, to others who need it. And people say Egypt is lost. Egypt can never be lost with people like you and Nadeem. Thanks, man!"

Osman extends his hand, his eyes full of gratitude. Ziko pauses speechless, he shakes hands with Osman; they briefly hug. Osman smiles, excuses himself and leaves. We hear him loudly welcoming the visitors and we spot him tapping the shoulders of his new team.

"Wow, I don't know whether I should be proud or ashamed," Ziko mumbles to himself.

All the way home, Ziko remains silent. Even when I try to throw in a joke here or there, he just smiles briefly. At home, Nadeem, Salma and Dr. Rashad are in the living room.

"What are you saying, Nadeem? Is that even possible?" Dr. Rashad asks.

"Apparently they worked out a deal with Bakry, a win-win deal," Nadeem says.

"You mean they threatened him," Salma corrects.

"What's going on?" Ziko asks.

"Turn of events in Bakry's case. Today in the morning, the charges against Bakry got dropped. He confessed that some terrorists threatened him to keep their guns in his new felucca, which coincidentally has been given to him by the internal forces. Actually it might have been the terrorists' intent because then it wouldn't render suspicious in the police eyes. Those terrorists had beaten him up when he refused to cooperate, hence the bruises in his face, the swelling in his jaws and the limping. The making of the arms was the same as the ones in Rafah but the serial numbers although close, didn't exactly match. He got offered a bail from the police if he could lead to the arrest of those terrorists. He did as he was told and they got arrested yesterday but they turned out to be secret agents of another country and for confidentially reasons this country and those agents' names could not be revealed. Bakry became a hero, he is released and the case got transferred to our intelligence department," Nadeem finishes.

"So tell me Nadeem, do the internal forces and national safety departments hire screen-writers or some sort of qualified authors to tailor for them cases like this, just so they sound believable?" Ziko asks sarcastically.

"I wonder if anyone can buy this story," Dr. Rashad says.

"I do, or used to," confesses Salma. They all look at her. "Well, the media confirms it and why would the internal forces and national safety departments fabricate convictions and throw innocent people behind bars?"

They don't answer. Ziko's eyes reveal bitterness; Rashad's eyes convey resentment; Nadeem's eyeballs freeze in their sockets emotionless.

"Oh, god, this is totally messed up," Salma shakes his head and covers her face.

"The internal forces and national safety are screwed up, but why did Bakry cooperate. I thought he was different. He went on with it just like my father did with my mom's way of running the family. I thought he was different," Salma hugs a pillow, folds her legs under her on the sofa and hides her face in the cushiony sofa-arm.

"Salma, I wish there is a simple explanation. This is real-life. Wahby's plan got screwed when I presented the report about the arms in Rafah. He knew then that I am capable of exposing him if Bakry remains in custody. He had to save his face and the entire department of internal forces. I hate to admit it, but releasing Bakry is an unspoken deal and a virtual hand-shake between Wahby and I," Nadeem says.

"Wow," we all say in a trio mix of: amazement, disbelief and disgust.

"But for what it's worth, maybe it'll make you feel better if you think about Bakry and how he feels right now. Because if you do, maybe your dream won't lie shattered on the ground," Nadeem says, Salma appears to be willing to listen and the three of us are just staring at our iron-man in disbelief. He can acknowledge feelings after all.

"Bakry always felt like a strong and free man. He was the only Captain who played Nubian tunes on his felucca. Yes, the terms of running his business weren't as straightforward as they should have been, but you can feel his dignity. He was proud of his origin and what he does for a living. He wanted to earn more, but he never wanted to be someone he isn't. He is probably a wreck by now. He has been abused and forced to lie by people who supposedly share the same identity. For someone like Bakry, he perceives them as people who carry his last name, because he deals with tourists and foreigners all the time. Now, you have to understand that Bakry isn't the first and won't be the last to live through such circumstances. But when someone has high pride, they tend to fall really bad," Nadeem explains.

We remain muted. The look in Salma's eyes paint devastation, but with a different shade, or so I see it.

*'So, explain to me something '*حبيبي*' – habiby' (my love), she was devastated when she was mad at Bakry, now she is devastated because she is mad at the police guy. Same feeling but tastes and looks different. You may be a poet after-all '*حبيبي*' – habiby' (my love), because no-one understands poets.'*

Thankfully Dr. Rashad interrupts my mother's constant encouragement.

"And remember, Salma, your mission dictates counter-attacking what Wahby did to Bakry."

Salma's lost eyes move from Nadeem to Dr. Rashad, before they tilt down and solidify into a vacant gaze. Tears crystallize inside them. She doesn't utter a word for five whole minutes. After which, she grabs her purse and rushes outside.

"Saad, I hear you like ice-cream," Dr. Rashad unexpectedly jokes.

"Mama" says Bassim excitedly.

"Let's go." The three of us leave, supposedly for ice cream.

At the port, we are racing to gulp our fast melting ice cream. Salma takes few steps forward and few steps backward before she approaches Bakry's felucca. He is sitting outside, his crew inside. "Out of order" sign is affixed on his felucca. His elbow rests on the edge of the felucca, his head leaning on his palm. He looks down in disdain.

"Captain Bakry," Salma calls. Bakry doesn't move or look at her.

"I came here to thank you. You demonstrate rare pride in who you are. You are a true man. We all know the deal between you and sergeant Wahby and no one believes that you've given in.

Being free and out here helps people like me, helps your crew, your family, your neighbors and everyone to learn from you. You didn't fear them; they feared you. They feared your sense of belonging and your pride that's why they couldn't keep you behind bars or prosecute you. Your bravery scared them and it is such courage that will make you re-operate your felucca with dignity and pride.

They aren't true Egyptians; you are. They have nothing to stick to but their power, which sooner or later will fade away, but you have your dignity and morals. They didn't break you; they tried but you were too stubborn and solid for them to break. Everyone here knows that and we are all proud of you."

Bakry looks at Salma for few minutes. He glances over to catch a glimpse of the other felucca operators, of his crew and of people walking by. His eyes push some tears forward but somehow they get retreated back to their home-glands. His half-open eyes widen, his back straightens, his palms turn to fists, and he stands-up, snatches the "Out of order" sign, and calls upon his crew…

"Come on men, let's hit those waves and tame that wind."

On the side Wahby stands guarded by a couple of young police youths. They are staring and smiling at Bakry. Bakry glares at them and spits on the ground. Captain Moustache and Captain Hook raises their thumbs for Bakry, his crew cheers and the sails are pulled.

Salma dislikes the spitting act but she smiles at Bakry and extends her hand to him. Bakry shakes her hand… "I'll name my coming daughter Salma. This is a true Egyptian name. I'd want to her to be pretty like you, and always proud of the blood that runs down her veins."

"It is an honor Captain Bakry, and who knows may be she'll grow up to be the president of Egypt one day," Salma says.

Captain Bakry smiles and nods; Pride crowns his head. Then he excuses himself and jumps aboard his felucca.

"Wow, I don't know whether I should be proud or ashamed," Salma mumbles.

The Tomb Opens

CHAPTER TWENTY

The Good Cop

At home, we catch Nadeem walking a Nubian man to the door… "I'll see what I can do," he says as the man leaves.

Back inside our apartment, "Ever since I represented Osman and Bakry at the court, I've been called by the people here in Aswan to answer some legal questions, issues and uncertainties," Nadeem says.

"Is this a bad thing or a good thing?" Salma inquires.

"I see, it goes hand-in-hand with your mission," Dr. Rashad says as he pours himself some green tea.

"I agree that it serves my mission, **IF** and only **IF** it is publicized; because only then one can identify its impact, which will be my proof to the Canadian Embassy folks. BUT if it gets publicized, then I can be accused of plotting against the regime or at the least I can be accused of planning a protest. A group of people with a leader talking about law and what is politically wrong equals (=) Conspiracy."

"This is nonsense," Salma comments, her tone aggravated.

"Welcome to Egypt. By the way, South America, Asia, and Africa are all saying Hi too," Ziko ridicules. Salma shakes her head in dismay.

"It is a corrupted and damaged world we live in. Why else would four people like us, coming from totally different backgrounds find that the only hope in life is to immigrate and engrave their names in a totally strange climate?" Ziko asks bitterly.

"So what are you going to do, Nadeem?" Dr. Rashad asks.

"I don't know. I seriously don't."

"You need legal publicity. And what does legal publicity mean? It means media," Dr. Rashad gestures widely with his arms as if on stage.

"Dr. Rashad, with all due respect, media isn't a feasible option. I am no reporter or journalist. I don't even personally know a reporter or a journalist. Media means propaganda, which is against the terms and conditions of the mission. No, media is not the answer here."

"Social Media, officer Nadeem. Not traditional media. It's a new era we live in today. Oh, dear lord," Dr. Rashad clarifies in frustration.

"Let me show you how," Dr. Rashad walks to his room where his laptop is setup. Nadeem hesitates a bit, avoids looking at any of us then obediently follows Dr. Rashad.

While Nadeem is locked in his boot camp with Dr. Rashad, Salma plays with Bassim some singing and guessing games. She places him on her lap and reads to him some books that she downloads off the Internet. Salma laughs as Bassim giggles. He tickles her and plays tricks on her. She responds in a very kind and motherly manner. Bassim hugs her tight, pretends to be scared and hides his head in her embrace. He warms up to her and I can sense he misses the mother he sees in her femininity.

Time passes; the sun gracefully descends from the center of the sky where it commands its ultimate heating power, and leans more towards the west. It looks as if the sun is determined to witness Dr. Rashad's plan for Nadeem. It refuses to drown asleep in the Nile. I can see its face turning red-orange as if furious that they are taking very long time.

The door opens and Dr. Rashad exits proudly. The sun catches a glimpse of Nadeem's exhausted face before it kisses our day goodnight. On the sofa, Bassim is asleep on Salma's lap, his head resting on her well-rounded female front gifts. Salma is asleep too, her head leaning gently on Bassim's head and her arms embracing him.

"The 'Good Cop Voice' is born. His website, facebook page, twitter account are all in place," Dr. Rashad announces in a hushed yet excited tone careful not to wakeup the sleepers, but eager to celebrate the achievement.

After dinner, Dr. Rashad teaches Salma and Ziko how to market for Nadeem's Good Cop online presence. "Remember, as a team, together we stand, together we fall, together we win and the winner takes it ALL," Dr. Rashad emphasizes.

In the morning, Salma, Ziko and Dr. Rashad leave. I stay at home, to keep Bassim entertained and allow time for Nadeem to focus and do the homework given to him by Dr. Rashad. I am not sure if Nadeem has been denied any rest time by Dr. Rashad. His bottom has remained glued to his chair, his eyes have been focused on the laptop, his fingers pointing and clicking fast and unstoppable.

I take away four cups of tea and coffee that die in boredom and turn cold as he diligently ignores them, while recording his voice and typing his words. The broom and dustpan sweep away the one sandwich he has made, which Bassim has playfully cut into pieces and has strewn its crumbs about all over the ground.

About six hours fly-by before the triplets return home. "Is he in there?" Dr. Rashad asks. "Almost all day, earphones on, microphone on and keyboard on," I reply.

"Well, we have talked to every stone in Aswan about the 'Good Cop Voice' and how it can help them know their rights and hold-up their heads high. People must be showering him with questions and spreading the word right about now," Ziko says.

"I want to listen to what he says," Salma requests.

"Here," Dr. Rashad plugs his smart phone to the speakers in the kitchen. He opens the 'Good Cop' website on his smart phone and clicks on 'Listen Live'. The question is pasted at the top of the webpage and Nadeem is talking. The triplets sit on the rounded table.

"Yes, I am an officer, an early-retiree police officer. The intent of this program is to educate civilians about what it is that our job entails and to answer any questions or uncertainties about the civil and criminal laws in Egypt. I may not have all the answers, so I do welcome the interjection of subject matter experts, former or current cops, who may be willing to call-in, join our conversation or type useful resources that can help ease and improve the listeners' understanding of the law enforcement in Egypt," Nadeem then pauses and we can sense a fainting sigh blowing in his microphone.

"To answer the posed question: No, Cops are not hired to abuse civilians. But cops are human beings, who can commit mistakes. In case of a mistake, it should be made aware of in order to rectify any power misuse. In your question you are asking me to share with you a story where a cop acted in a noble manner. I am sure there are plenty of examples and I can sense that you are losing faith in the police service, so here - let me share with you this story. It is a true story. It is the story of an active officer – named Mahmoud who served in the internal affairs sector.

Mahmoud's job was to clean the streets of the city from the homeless and the potential suspects. It included putting down any protest or demonstration lest it could yield to any un-peaceful or chaotic results. Mahmoud was a qualified officer as the book dictated. He was very firm and didn't accept other than obedience when he ordered, after all that's what he was taught.

One night a colleague of his, had a commotion with a homeless woman. He contacted Mahmoud for backup. Mahmoud advised that such neighborhood was supposed to be cleared of all homeless in preparation for the president's march to pass by and that his colleague should take all drastic measures to attain this.

But the woman refused to cooperate or leave her spot, she screamed and shouted and demanded her right to stay as a free woman. Amid the swivel of shouting, pushing and shoving, an aimless bullet left an undetermined gun and the woman fell dead on the ground.

Mahmoud rushed to the scene. A bare-footed fifteen-month-old boy dressed in rags, walked wobbly towards the woman 'mama, mama' he called his mama, but his mother turning fast blue didn't answer him back. 'Mama' he called again but still no answer. The boy knelt down, put his tiny hand on his mother's body, somewhere between the heart and the stomach, then looked back at his hand tainted and colored red with fresh warm blood. The boy looked around and his eyes met Mahmoud's. The boy looked at Mahmoud, his eyes questioning… why his mama wasn't answering, 'mama, mama', and why his hand is all red. And how can Mahmoud possibly explain? Well there was really no good explanation for the boy to lose his mother who had nothing but her spot on the street to fight for and demand the right to keep. The boy attempted to lick his hand, that's when Mahmoud left the scene hurriedly.

The boys' eyes hunted Mahmoud in his days and nights. He had instructions to follow. He cascaded the orders down and enforced them without a touch of reason or patience.

It rendered a hard lesson for Mahmoud. He made sure the boy got put for adoption by good parents. He learned that society without a good cop turns wild and savage; however society with a bad cop also turns wild and savage.

Here is a message from Mahmoud to all the cops out there… "Watch out fellows, we start off brave, good-willed and devoted but it is dark out there, slippery and foggy. If we can't stop, find a mirror and look at ourselves, we'll wake up on a hideous version of ours… arrogant, egocentric who would do anything to impose their will and vision on others; incapable of seeing others as equals, or treating them with respect. We'll become highly combative and intimidating. We'll interpret everything as a test of wills, and we won't be able to back down.

Watch-out fellows, our road is bumpy. Don't walk with a club in your hand, lifting your nose in the air, you won't see under your feet and sooner or later you'll trip and fall.

Fellow listeners, using threats and reprisals to get obedience from others and to keep them off-balance and insecure is not and will never be approved by any law. Know your borders and respect them, others will respect you for it. Know your law and act accordingly."

The guy thanks Nadeem. Despite the small screen of Dr. Rashad's smart phone, he points at the increasing number of listeners that was shooting hundreds every minute.

"Thanks for listening. Please call us at: (+20) 97/2315789 to share your story, or contact the email address below with your inquiry."

Salma covers her mouth with both her hands; tears run down her face. Ziko looks down and shakes his head. Nadeem emerges from his room and checks on Bassim on the sofa. He plants a kiss on the kid's cheek. Bassim smiles, opens his eyes, winks at his father, and then moves inside his embrace curling his tiny arms around his father's back, but failing to close them in a hug.

"Bassim is the little boy on your talk-show, isn't he? That's why he keeps calling his mother. That's why he doesn't say anything else, right?" Salma shouts and cries.

Nadeem looks at all of us in shock. He places Bassim on his lap and embraces him…"Bassim is my son and till the day I die, he'll be my son. His mother was his only family. I adopted him; and for him I retired; and for him I'll immigrate. I don't want him to grow up, hearing rumors that his dad might have been involved in killing his biological mother. I love Bassim as my own son. Daddy loves you, Bassim. You know that, right?"

"Mama"

Salma runs to her room. Dr. Rashad fixes his eyeglasses on his nose then walks off to his room. I stay in the kitchen. Nadeem forces a smile on his face to please Bassim.

"Take it easy on yourself, Nadeem. Not a lot of people would have done what you did," Ziko says.

"I don't know whether I should be proud or ashamed," Nadeem replies.

The Tomb Opens

CHAPTER TWENTY ONE

Transformed

My new disability loosens my grip on the driving wheel and lifts my now-soft foot off the gas and brake pedals. Days slip from my grasp like water, and calendar papers flip and peel faster than my realization. I give up my chauffeur's role to Dr. Rashad and take my seat as a passenger.

It is the first time I feel that I am not in control. I never felt that driving is too much or that being a taxi driver is a tedious job, except when I got stuck in traffic. It was my wings that took me places I wouldn't have visited otherwise. But hey, doctors said it is temporary so I am going to suck it up, live through it and enjoy being the lazy observant.

Dr. Rashad calls for a break from the mission-related activities, "One leisure outing, then back to work, every bee in its own hive".
I take the seat in the front.

"I never really opted for driving. But in Aswan, I find it tolerable," Dr. Rashad says, suffocating my driving wheel with his squeezing hands and his too much leaning-forward body.

I find myself developing a new appreciation for my rear mirror. Dr. Rashad tilts it towards him and rids me the opportunity to see the reflection of the scenery on the passengers in the back, their eye contact, unvoiced feelings and nonverbal communication. Oh God, my rear mirror has given me in-depth look from so many different angels, nurtured my insights and added colour to my world of streets, bridges, people and underground roads. Without it, any trip is plain and boring. Interesting, one feels the significance of something only after losing it.

'You mourn over your rear mirror more than you ever mourned over losing me' – Always alive in my heart and especially in my head, Ma.

"Mama, pee pee."

Dr. Rashad pulls over at the closest potentially clean toilet location, the Cataract hotel. Nadeem takes Bassim in. Dr. Rashad's bladder shows the same interest as Bassim's, so he follows them. We leave the car. Salma checks the accessories displayed at the small booths in the lobby.

"Interesting…" Ziko points at a minivan parking in front of us, from which a group of musicians start to descend. Ziko's eyes shine at the sight of the lady holding a violin case.

"Excuse me, Mademoiselle"

"Yes," she wears her auburn hair short – a'la garcon-ish. She has few freckles and very shy dimples. A navy polo shirt hugs her upper torso and a pair of beige Capri pants falls seamlessly to cover two-thirds of her calves. She carries her violin case by a strap resting on her right shoulder.

"My two-year old nephew rushed inside the lobby to the toilet. I checked the men's room but he isn't there. Could you be kind as to check the ladies room? I am worried about him."

"Sure, no problem," she walks inside. Ziko smiles and checks his wristwatch.
Nadeem comes out. Bassim is strolling happily beside him.

"Bassim, some ice-cream buddy?" Ziko offers.

Bassim abandons his father's hand and holds Ziko's. Nadeem paints a smile, and Ziko walks inside the hotel. I peek and I see him talking to the violinist, pointing at Bassim, then shaking her hand and heading towards the ice-cream fridge. A couple of minutes later, Bassim tugs gently with his small hand on the violinist shirt and offers her an ice-cream sandwich, before he runs back to Ziko. She smiles at Ziko, who smiles back then winks. They maintain eye contact for a minute or so. Then he races Bassim outside the lobby to where we are.

"She is still looking, isn't she?" he asks me.

"Timidly, but yes," I answer.

He smiles, lifts Bassim up and starts playing with him. The more Bassim giggles, the more she smiles.

"Let's go," Dr. Rashad says picking up his pace as he comes out of the hotel. Salma stuffs her small purchases in her purse. Ziko pretends not to notice the violinist any more. We take our seats. Then suddenly but naturally believable Ziko's eyes move as they glance around casually and again meet the violinist's eyes. He smiles and locks their gazes together until our spinal cords ache in pain as we hit the back of our seats when Dr. Rashad steps vigorously on the gas pedal.

"Ouch," Salma says. Bassim giggles.

Dr. Rashad prefers walking to driving, "It is a sport, it gives you the chance to observe, it helps the massive intake of oxygen, only in Cairo it helps the massive intake of carbon-monoxide".

On the days I accompany Ziko, we go to new places like Abu Simbel. We take a tour bus to go there because it's three hours away and if Dr. Rashad drives, we'll all die of nervous breakdown.

Ziko comes a long way. His speeches about Aswan and Luxor, their culture, language, people's qualities and heritage become so polished that it has attracted some reporters from various channels local and international. They tape it, conduct personal interviews with him and pose for taking pictures with tourists gathered around him.

"Are you a tour guide," they ask.

"I am just an Egyptian, passionate about his culture. People here are warm and friendly. There is no place like Aswan."

It intrigues me that such simple words draw a smile on Aswanians' faces and engrave a sense of pride in their hearts. That's what I overhear them saying when they point at him.

Ziko looks especially sharp in his newly grown and handsomely groomed beard and moustache. Walking with him now feels like walking with a celebrity, only a celebrity who stops, shakes hand with everyone and asks them about their day, "How wonderful is your day, today?" Ziko can run for a mayor here and without campaigns he'll be offered the throne.

I join Nadeem occasionally too. He tells me about the vast and endless responses on his 'Good Cop Voice' Internet channel.

"The messages and questions just won't stop. Dr. Rashad created a database for it, to save me from answering the repeated questions."

The phone line in our apartment has undergone several episodes of heart attack, and we can see sergeant Wahby's finger prints written all over it. So Nadeem has switched to using his cell phone.

Nadeem's program had made him a legend. Numerous calls, stories, doubts, inquiries have come his way and have pled for guidance and understanding. "It's all about education," Dr. Rashad keeps repeating, "Dictators and corruption only thrive in illiterate nations."

People stop and greet Nadeem as we go. They rave about his voice that rings loud and clear...

"'The Good Cop' show presents you with the following topics: 1) Expressed Intentions, how to see them, understand them and be prepared to what's next; 2) Hidden Intentions, how to look out for them, be aware of them and prepare yourself for the unknown; 3) The No-Profiling – Yet – Cat's Eye attitude; 4) Difference between Threats and Negatives Attitudes:

Stealing Monuments is a Threat, while Touting is a Negative Attitude; 5) Restore Accountability; and finally 6) Earn Trust & Respect."

Under the guidance of Dr. Rashad, Nadeem has tailored the content on his show to attract both civilians and law-enforcement personnel.

"The nation that has its law-enforcement personnel and civilians on the same team is undefeatable. Its internal structure is robust and impenetrable," Dr. Rashad has guided and instructed, Nadeem has listened and applied.

Unlike Ziko, Nadeem declines all interview requests with reporters; "Inside me is still a police officer, very rare that you find a police officer posing for a camera take."

The most tiring yet exciting of them all is tagging along with Salma, "It's clear for me what I want to accomplish but it isn't clear for me, how to accomplish it".

She talks with poets and scriptwriters. She visits villages and farmland in Aswan, takes pictures and mingles with people. She spends the night visiting all entertainment arenas in hotels, restaurants, and nightclubs, her cell phone shooting pictures and her pen running on her notepad.

I knock on her room one day and I am amazed at the huge wooden board she hangs up on the wall and the amount of sticky notes and pictures that grow and overflow off the board to cover all her bedroom walls from the hip-level to slightly above the eye-level.

"Poor this child," Dr. Rashad says.

"I know, I wish we can help her," Ziko sympathizes.

"See, each one of us has interacted with the world from a certain angle. Her problem is that she has been in a bubble all her life. Her bubble didn't even allow her to see but those people sharing the same bubble. She has no clue as of how to find a place for herself in the real world. And if you can't find a place for yourself, you'll never fit in," Dr. Rashad elaborates.

"At least, we show our support and tell her that we are here for her," Nadeem suggests.

"She needs to interact with people, yet stay wrapped. She needs to reach their hearts and minds, yet remain looking from behind a sheer film or layer. This layer is transparent enough for others to communicate wit her through, yet stretchy, malleable and unbreakable to protect and shield her; I am thinking something like Lycra," Dr. Rashad thinks out loud, his palm cupping his chin, his index finger tapping on his face, and his eyes looking outside his glasses to the side and onto an empty space.

The one face that I usually see everywhere I turn when I am with either one of them is sergeant Wahby's. It is like he is cloned three times. I vaguely remember what he said the night Nadeem and I were swimming the Nile River but I know it wasn't good.

Ziko and Nadeem become good friends. They talk, walk and play the famous Egyptian dice-game TAWALA together.

"Marriage wasn't one of my options. Girlfriend after the other left because of my stubborn nature and non-negotiable orders. But it didn't bother me much. I enjoyed hopping from one flower to another, taking enough of the scent it has, then flying again free without any commitment cuffs," Nadeem jokes with Ziko.

"After healing from my failed-marriage attempt, I've always been the cool guy around females. But there is this one girl, that I find myself all clumsy and speechless around," Ziko confesses.

"Who is the lucky girl?"

"Mona, the violinist. Fate knitted a trap for me to meet her here in Aswan. I go with Salma on the nights she goes to the Cataract just to see her playing. I praise her talent after the show but then my blabbing tongue stays glued to the top of my mouth and words desert my dictionary. She throws me some leads, but I just nod or smile, like a dumb male-Barbie doll."

"Wow, this is old-times love my friend," Nadeem laughs.

"I know, but I just can't help it. It's like a fever."

"We're expanding our efforts; Tomorrow new locations, new people, new challenges. Let's get some sleep now." Dr. Rashad turns off the lights.

"Well, if it isn't for papa, who will tuck us in?" Ziko starts to joke when Salma screams and turns the lights of the living room back on.

"I got it,"

"What?" Dr. Rashad asks.

"I want to do something for each and everyone who helped me here in Aswan. I've been doing a lot of thinking. People here in Aswan, have been neglected by the government. They feel no attachment what so ever. If it weren't for the monuments, they'd probably forgotten the name EGYPT all together. But you can't ask a kid to feel attached to a mother than doesn't see him or pay attention to him. I want to bring the Aswanian people in the spot light, No; I want to bring the spot light to them."

"Are you thinking about leading a protest? Because, that's not..." Nadeem inquires.

"More like a revolution. But in a musical play format. A revolutionary musical play to highlight the issues and needs of the Aswanians and at the same time fix the missing link between them and the bigger Egypt."

Salma goes on and on. At the beginning they are all looking at her in sympathy as if she has lost her sanity. However by the time she finishes laying out her plan, they are looking at her in amazement. Her eyes are wide open, her neck is stretched up, her hands are doing all kinds of open and close, expand and contract gestures; and Bassim is climbing her back and pulling her ear-lobe.

"Brilliant, Salma, You've found your Lycra. But this needs a lot of work and research."

"Research, I did. Work, I am determined to do it, papa and I will."

"Salma my dear, research is never done. It is an ongoing activity. Let's say you are done the part that gets you started. Carry on, my dear," Dr. Rashad emphasizes.

"I am ready, I am so ready, ---- But I need help."

I look in the living room and I see four different people. Something inside them gets kindled and throws its glare on their faces. Even little Bassim, seems a lot happier.

'Saad 'حبيبي – habiby' (my love), you know when you start philosophizing, it only means one thing: you're ready to find your pillow and call it a day.' – Ah, that lovely voice again.

"OK, people, we'll pick it up tomorrow. Good night" Dr. Rashad draws the heavy curtains on the day. I wonder if he's overheard my mom's voice.

The Tomb Opens

CHAPTER TWENTY TWO

Show Time and Pay Back

Nadeem and Ziko's reputation facilitates the access to the 'Great Temple of Ramses II' for Salma's showcase at 10:00 PM, on October the 21st, 2010. This night coincides with Mr. Saqr's scheduled visit.

My arm and leg are finally cast free. We enter the temple at 6:00 PM and I look at his majesty, Ramses II, seated with his hands on his thighs. The young, handsome face is finely carved. He wears a double crown on his head and a heavy nemes flares out on both sides of his face. The line of the smiling lips is more than a meter long.

Dr. Rashad shakes hands with Mr. Saqr. Bassim and I are backstage witnessing the rehearsals, the costumes, the lights and the orchestra. Ziko's face lights up as he spots Mona among the musicians. The entire place is bustling with action. People are carrying things, constructing props, rolling theatre furniture, extending cables, checking curtains, and adjusting spotlights. Nadeem comes and checks on Bassim about 35 times. The last few times, Bassim doesn't recognize him because of the make-up that has dramatically changed his looks.

"What? I am a police officer. I am not a performer and if it weren't for the sake of working together as a team, I would have **NEVER** put on such a mask, clothes or did what I am about to do up there," Nadeem says furiously but in a hushed tone. Then he turns and leaves.

At 10:00 p.m. sharp, the curtains open on a large tomb, lying flat in the middle of the stage. A deep voice echoes loudly saying… " 'The Tomb Opens' welcomes you all" … followed by some scary sound effects.

Dr. Rashad hops on the stage, holds a microphone and says…"It's with great regret that Egypt had lost three of her citizens: Salma, Nadeem and

Ziko. They weren't lost to an accident, a tragic event or death. It was their decision to leave Egypt and look for another motherland to adopt them. In this tomb, their bodies sleep and in an hour their souls will fly away to their new motherland.

On the other side of the stage, in her dark skin and slender body, stands Egypt. She's ready to wave goodbye to them. The green scarf in her hand is also ready to gracefully brush away the tears of loss." Dr. Rashad stops. The spot lights land on the Egypt lady. Dr. Rashad descends the stage and takes his seat next to Mr. Saqr.

"So long Salma, So long Nadeem, So long Ziko, with all the love I have for you, I want you to stay and I hate to see you leave," the Egypt lady says and with the scarf, she brushes away her tears.

The stage lights dim. The stage itself shakes. The tomb in the middle turns hard. Its cover flips open and flame comes out of it like a volcano has just been erupted.

Amid the smoke, three bodies slowly rise from the tomb, all dressed like pharaohs. Some lights shed on the walls where monuments are setup and hieroglyphs are engraved in the walls.

"Where are we?" Ziko asks.
"Are we there yet?" Nadeem asks.
"Don't think so. Mother Egypt didn't wave to us yet. Is it possible that we missed her waving?" Salma asks.

Then all of a sudden the stage brightens up with lights and a group of dancers enter… "Aswan, the land of gold; Aswan, the history, Aswan, forever you'll behold….," the singing and the folk dancing start.

Men and women wear colorful outfits. Women wear gowns and have their hair done in braids peeping out of the green headscarves dangling from their heads and along their backs. Men wear loose-fit white pants and shirts. They dance as a group.

The music lively engages the audience who start clapping. The style is very unique and joyful. They do hobble-step or limping-step; then top it with relaxed arm sweeps and cross-movements and slightly bent torsos. Group of dancers finish then another group starts. Different dances yet same lyrics:

> My kid is sick, doctors hear just never answer
> Need a surgery, hospital gates have no grasper?
> Have to study, electricity is a breakage
> Fruits and Veggies, watered by sewage
> Aswan heritage we'll behold
> Job opportunities for us, never unfold
> Aswan, the land of gold
> Aswan, the history, you'll behold
> You at the top, hope you are listening
> Aswan people are calling for help

The crowd starts following the rhythms. The lyrics are distributed in flyers among the audience. Everyone begins to sing along:

> My kid is sick, doctors hear just never answer
> Need a surgery, hospital gates have no grasper?
> Have to study, electricity is a breakage
> Fruits and Veggies, watered by sewage
> Aswan heritage we'll behold
> Job opportunities for us, never unfold
> Aswan, the land of gold
> Aswan, the history, you'll behold
> You at the top, hope you are listening
> Aswan people are calling for help

The last group finishes their dance and the lights spot on the three in the tomb.

"I have pain in my stomach" Salma says.
"My legs can't move" Ziko says.
"I can't put my finger on it, but I'm pretty sure, I'm leaving something behind. I just hope I don't remember it after it's too late" Nadeem says.

Another sound echoes from the other side of the stage… "Welcome to your new motherland. I'm here to pick you up and I know you've been waiting for this moment your entire life. Let's go. Shed those ancient looks of yours and let's put on some modern ones."

"Bye Salma, Bye Ziko, Bye Nadeem," Egypt says. The stage darkens immensely, the tomb turns vigorously.

"My soul, it's trying to break free and fly," shouts Ziko.
"Mine too," affirms Nadeem.
Salma doesn't say anything but her panting is heard all over. "NO" she cries. "NO, I can't go."
"Me neither" said Nadeem and Ziko.

The tomb stops turning. The three of them wobble their way out of it and run to Egypt who hugs them all.
"You really want to stay?"
"With you, we'll stay, for you, for Aswan, for all of us, for all of us."

The show takes four hours with three intermission periods. When the show ends, the crowd stands and the applause shakes the walls of the theatre for five whole minutes. Mr. Saqr applauds. With Bassim's little hand in mine, I look at the crowd, then back at the team. All is happy, all is proud.

The activity in the temple entrance carries on till 5:00 in the morning with people gathering around the team, talking, celebrating and taking pictures. Nadeem smiles conservatively and doesn't talk much. People start leaving and Dr. Rashad decides to take Bassim back to the apartment … "I am an old man and this child needs to rest."

Mr. Saqr offers to give Dr. Rashad and Bassim a ride. I carry sleepy Bassim to the car. I return back to find the place has been deserted. I hardly catch up with the team.

"They have been invited to celebrate their performance in a special party. A police officer escorted them. They went in that direction," Mona tells me as she and her fellow musicians pack their instruments.

As I follow the direction and I go deeper inside the temple. I don't see or hear anyone. It gets creepier as I make my way through numerous narrow and twisted allies. I lose hope in finding them, so I decide to exit this cavern.

But every turn I take, I find a blockage path. I turn again but no luck. "Hello" I call out. But it's the hollow land. My echo comes back and rings in my ears. I sit for some time, trying to think about how they'll find me. Then I rise again and go against my instinctive map. I take different paths and I feel I am going up the temple from inside. Then I hear a laugh, loud and clear. It isn't Nadeem, Salma's or Ziko's. It is Wahby's.

I don't know where I am or how I ended up here, but I can see them down from where I stand, at quite a distance, surrounded by five bulky men and Wahby. I stand, motionless and speechless.

"Impressive, really impressive," Wahby applauds.
"You must have been in the drama club when you were in police college," Wahby mocks Nadeem.

"I have to congratulate you all, on an awesome job. You know for educated people like yourselves who claim to be interested in history, you are quite illiterate.

Have you heard about **Khaled Saeed***. He too was ambitious as to straighten things out, and he foolishly underestimated the players he was versing. At the age of 28 in Alexandria, he got arrested by the security forces and he never emerged alive again. Photos of his disfigured corpse after his arrest have spread throughout the internet. This should have been a lesson for anyone like him who thinks he can stand in face of the policing style in Egypt. But what can I say?

Here you are, and since you chose Aswan, then you must be familiar with the mummification process. First your bodies will be cut open and your organs will be kept in jars. Then special chemical preservatives will be pasted on your bodies and you'll be wrapped in warm fine linen sheets. How about we start with the lady?"

* Murder of Khaled Saeed at the hands of police is a true story — June 6, 2010

Wahby pulls Salma's hand. Nadeem pushes him away and Ziko punches him. Four bulky men start scoring against Nadeem and Ziko brutally until they fall on their knees. The fifth bully holds Salma by the hair and punches her every time she screams "Stop".

Wahby shouts like a maniac, "**What? You thought I gave up?** I told you Nadeem, it isn't over. I just liked your little game so I enjoyed watching you chasing your own tail and wrapping yourself in your own mummy dress.

Now gentlemen, I want you to execute mummification on our guests. They love Aswan and they have to be buried in it, I can't really think of a better ending to your show on stage and off stage other than that," Wahby signals to his helpers, each snaps a large sharp blade, waves it, then holds it high and launches an attack on Ziko and Nadeem, while yelling "HA".

'It kind of reminds you of the brave heart movie, doesn't it' – not now, Ma, please.

I hear Salma screaming.

But then a strong light suddenly penetrates the temple all the way to the inner sanctum. The gangsters freeze, their arms still hanging in the air in the attack position. Wahby turns instantly pulling his gun out. All the eyes widen, examining the source of light. The light is coming their way, it bounces off their blades and gets harshly reflected on their faces. Their eyes are instantly blinded but mine aren't. I look on the other side. And it seems to me as if it is sun rays, coming from a slit in the wall of the temple. But something is there next to this slit, something like a pipe, a long narrow shiny pipe. A series of bullets leave the pipe. They are targeted, they are aim-full and they get masterfully planted in Wahby's and his men's arms and legs. The horror show ends.

I try not to look directly at the light, but instead to make sense of what's around it. As the figure I see moves a bit, the sniper looms clearer to me. He has a head-cover. He examines the scene through the lens of his gun. He is content by his accomplished mission. He pulls back his gun, opens a case and places it inside it. Then he snaps off his elastic dark head-cover. He turns, No, she turns. The sniper is a She. She places the strap of her case on her right shoulder and climbs her way out. This strapping style reminds me of someone, but who?

"Nadeem, Ziko, answer me," Salma cries but apparently can't move. I have to go call someone, if I ever made it out of this maze-like temple.

The Tomb Opens

CHAPTER TWENTY THREE

Sniper – friend or foe

Back in Cairo, we meet with Mr. Saqr by the swimming pool of one of the hotels in Maadi.

"It is a fact, the axis of the temple is positioned by the ancient Egyptian architects in such a way that twice a year, on October 22 and February 22, the rays of the sun penetrate the sanctuary and illuminate the sculpture on the back wall, except for the statue of 'Ptah', the god connected with the Underworld, who always remains in the dark. The penetration starts at 6:25 am and lasts for 24 minutes. These dates are allegedly the king's birthday and coronation day respectively. So you were just lucky and they were certainly cursed by some ancient Egyptian's god," Dr. Rashad explains.

"The investigations are still being conducted. Wahby and his men are being convicted, but they are injured badly. I wonder who the sniper might be." Nadeem asks.

"Well, it is either Dr. Rashad or Saad, because they weren't with us," mocks Salma.

"I wish it was me," says Dr. Rashad, looking at Ziko's and Nadeem's deformed faces and their casted limbs.

"Anyway, congratulations, you did an excellent job on your missions. Within six to nine months you'll have your visa," announces Mr. Saqr, his eyebrows hang up; his grin grows wider revealing his chipmunk-like teeth. He excuses himself and leaves, "I'll be in touch".

"This is a nice place Ziko, why did you pick it as our meeting place," Nadeem teases.

"It has a stimulating musical ambiance."

I look at the stage and I see Mona playing her violin. They all smile and look back at Ziko. Her eyes flash an image for me, a horrifying image though. But it can't be, can it?

"Mama, vroom, vroom" Bassim says as he tries to fly a paper-plane. He then climbs Nadeem's legs and sits on his lap. Nadeem hugs him, opens his hands and looks intently at the paper-plane before he unfolds it. The paper has lines of heliographies. Salma reads Nadeem's suspicions. She opens her smart phone and Nadeem dictates the symbols. Ziko writes the translated letters on the receipt then he reads the words out loud…

I just want you to know that you are not under any sort of formal protection. That morning your agenda matched mine; that's why I intervened. This isn't always going to be the case. If we happen to meet again, I might be on the other side of the table. Just hope you know what you are doing and why – if we happen to cross-paths again in life.

The sniper

The sniper's words mute everyone for few long minutes.

"It is good thing we are immigrating then," Ziko breaks the silence.

Dr. Rashad stands, "Well, I guess this is it. It was really nice getting to know you all. See, I lived with my wife for 30 years. I lost her six years ago. I'd always complained about her being too social. While she'd seen something worthy in each and every person she'd met, I just encountered ridiculous, void, self-centered, nosy, obnoxious figures that looked like human beings.

My life has become really vacant without her. I have my brother and my nephew as my only family now. They are in Alexandria. After I land in Canada, I'll sponsor them both.

I just want to say that when I first met you, I saw absolutely no potential in anyone of you. Honest to god, you all represented the indictment of the Egyptian education system and an ultimate degradation in culture, ethics, and the list goes on. I honestly felt both sad and disgusted. But I don't know how this changed along the way. Not just how each one of you developed but how my feelings towards you all, developed too.

When Saad called, I was trying to make sense of his words through his hysterical tone. Then the scene that was waiting for me as I arrived at the temple: the two of you bleeding unconsciously on the floor, I could almost swear that I saw parts of your flesh lying vulnerably on the ground; and Salma beaten cruelly. I felt like a papa-bear who is ready to take your attackers down by one blow of his claws. I guess all I am trying to say is that… I mean, I just want to say that…" Dr. Rashad's intelligence struggles then fails to lend him any more words.

Salma hugs Dr. Rashad while Nadeem and Ziko position their crutches and hardly make it to their feet, joining the group hug.

"And remember it all about…"

"Education" together they complete his sentence. They laugh, and Dr. Rashad beams with a smile.

The Tomb Opens

CHAPTER TWENTY FOUR

New Year - 2011

I miss them together. Each one calls me and I drive them here and there, but they don't meet together, at least not with me around. I accompany Salma to schools and day cares where she volunteers her time and talks to children about Egypt, "I figured with the knowledge I have, I can maybe just impress kids. But every day I learn more. Dr. Rashad sends me all kinds of links and resources."

I accompany Nadeem to his physiotherapy sessions and baby-sit Bassim who can now say: "Daddy".

I meet with Ziko at Café settings where live-bands play, "Finally, I mastered the courage to tell her I have a crush on her. She kisses me on the cheek, says that it is because she really cares for me that she doesn't want to have a relationship. What does this suppose to mean?"

Something in me swears that Mona is the sniper but another voice cautions me that it may have been hallucinations. I want to tell Ziko but I remain muted.

It is December 31, 2010 – new year eve. Cairo is illuminating in its velvety dress diamonded with lights. Yes, officially Egypt doesn't celebrate New Year eve, but we, Egyptians just love any excuse to party. One day I'll spend New Year eve in Dahab. I hear it is legendary. Anyway, people get pretty generous around this time of the year, which is a great reason to celebrate the event.

But sadly my hopes in making good money evaporate upon receiving an urgent call from Ziko. I rush to meet him at 2:00 in the morning, January 1, 2011. He is accompanied by Nadeem and Salma.

"The Coptic Church in Alexandria got bombed at Midnight*. I called papa numerously to check on his family there, but received no answer. We have to go."

We stop by Dr. Rashad's apartment in Cairo first and after awakening all the neighbors by our door banging, we make our way to Alexandria. It feels as if we own the roads, as there is absolutely nobody there at this hour, which highly contradicts with the scene we spot as we stop by the church.

I stay with Bassim while Ziko, Nadeem, and Salma navigate the area through the police and the ambulance. They look in every face. No sign of Dr. Rashad. We leave to various hospitals to check on the admitted wounded people. They rush inside each hospital then they rush back outside. Dr. Rashad is nowhere to be found. It is both relieving and scary.

"Nadeem, we need a permission to see those who were announced dead at the scene," Ziko says. Nadeem sighs, "I'll see what I can do."

We leave sleepy Bassim with a nurse and run down a long corridor in one of the hospitals. We spot Dr. Rashad sitting on one of chairs, shaking his head and looking at the ground, his glasses have fallen off his face and are lying broken on the floor.

"Dr. Rashad," the three of them gather around him.

"My brother and nephew are both dead. My entire family is gone. They got killed, at the same time, same place while praying. Why? Why would anyone do something like this? Who kills people when they worship and pray? Who does that? Why? Who kills praying people? Why?" he cries. Salma sobs. Nadeem and Ziko pat his shoulders.

After an hour, Bassim cries and I take him back to the cab. I doze-off behind my driving wheel. They spend the night with Dr. Rashad inside the hospital; until they step-out as the sun lazily stretch its rays across the horizon.

* True Story

"Saad, please drive to the closest hotel and stop for some breakfast, will you?"

Ziko turns to Nadeem and asks: "Do you think this is a religious-based attack, you know, 'the Muslim Christian fiasco'?"

"No, This is one of the cases, where the 'WHO DID IT - PERSON' doesn't carry the same motivation as the 'WHY DO IT - PERSON'. Remember, this is Alexandria. Khaled Saeed's murder is still on people's hearts and minds. It has created a volcano of anger than is about to erupt at any time. Fumes of rage are coming from every corner and every hole. Now, what makes people forget a tragedy?"

"A bigger tragedy," Ziko replies.

"Exactly, but with different people to point the blaming fingers at," Nadeem finishes.

"Rats, more than 20 died and almost 100 injured," Ziko snaps. Nadeem doesn't reply. Salma listens, shaking her head, dropping tears and patting on Bassim's head that lies peacefully on her lap.

As we munch on our sandwiches, a marching demonstration invades the streets with signs reading "**Together, we'll die together, or live together***". College and university students dominate the streets condemning the brutal attack on the church and declaring their unified existence as one Muslim/Christian community.

Ziko and Nadeem buy Dr. Rashad some food, some clothes and some personal hygienic items. In two hours we are back at the hospital. They shave him, dress him and get him to eat. They accompany him through the funeral and burying process.

"On January 7, I'll be there at the church, celebrating Christmas. I don't care if I get killed. I should have been with my brother and nephew right now," Dr. Rashad agonizes.

* True Story

Dr. Rashad decides to stay in Alexandria. We stay too. Bassim spends the night on January 6 with Salma at the hotel. Ziko, Nadeem and I accompany Dr. Rashad to the church and observe the chanting and prayers. Shoulder to shoulder we remain. The church is filled with both Muslims and Christians. The morning wakes up on people marching again on the streets, **"Together, we'll die together, or live together*"**.

At dinner, Bassim gives each one of us a napkin then climbs a chair and rubs his buttocks in, until he feels completely seated. Dr. Rashad's grief is colored more by sadness than anger now. His new eyeglasses that Ziko has bought, give him a totally different cool look.

"I don't know what to say, I've lost my brother and my nephew and I've earned three sons, a daughter and a grandson."

"We love you, papa," Salma says.

"Without your harsh, whip-like lesson, I wouldn't have done the Good Cop Voice. Do you know it is still on and active, very active actually? I don't know if I'll be able to administer it after I land in Canada."

"Without you, none of us would have accomplished their mission. You helped each and every one of us. It is all because of your theories. An insightful brain like yours knows better than blaming any religion for burning the church, Right?" Ziko says unexpectedly.

"Ziko, not the time" Salma and Nadeem scold him.

"That's OK. I know, Ziko. Yes, there are and will always be efforts to bang the two religions against each other and there are people who are extremists in both religions that help such efforts succeed. At the end, a civil conflict or war is guaranteed to destroy any nation. But it is all coming from people; I will never blame a holy reference for humanity suffering. All that is necessary for evil to prevail is for all good men to do nothing."

"Well said, papa," Ziko replies. Nadeem and Salma glare at Ziko.

"What? Well, I don't know about you two, but since Mona expressed no interest in joining me, then once we land in Canada, I am contacting each one of you. We've become inseparable. And for me to keep liking someone, I need to be at peace with them and carry no hard feelings. So I wanted to get this out of the way and off our chests, once and for all."

"Ha, Ha," Dr. Rashad laughs.

"You are actually laughing papa, come-on we need to see a doctor, waiter please call an ambulance," Ziko jokes.

"Ha, Ha," Dr. Rashad laughs again. Bassim looks at him in worry and hides his face with his small chubby hands.

The Tomb Opens

CHAPTER TWENTY FIVE

The 25th January Revolutionary Roar

Late the same month of January 2011, on the 25th, the human head of Sphinx lets out a loud roar that strikes the world, and millions of Egyptians walk down the streets of Egypt asking for a chance in life, demanding to be treated with humanity, asking for dignity, freedom and social justice. Tahrir square is filled with aspiring hearts and determined souls.

Upon Mr. Saqr's request I pick-up the team, and head towards the Canadian embassy. Mr. Saqr calls my cell phone and his voice runs loud and clear on the speaker: "Listen folks, because your process has already started, we can request for you to get the Visa at the airport and leave instantly. Or we can wait until it takes its scheduled time to finish. But it may be delayed because of this unrest. This is a case of emergency and we can expedite things. What do you guys think?"

"Expedite,"

"Expedite, yes, certainly,"

"Yeah, sure,"

"I can't hear you loud enough," Mr. Saqr says. He is right; the sound of the massive amount of people on the streets walking towards Tahrir Square makes the individual's voice sounds like the squeaking of a tiny mouse.

"Ok, call me when you get to a quieter place and better reception," he hangs up.

I can't drive any further. The road is blocked.

"I'll go and watch," Ziko says.

"Me too," Salma says.

"Yes, me too," Dr. Rashad hesitates but follows.

"You don't have to wait here Saad, you are a free man and if you want to participate, you should, just lock the cab," Nadeem tells me.

"What about you, now that Bassim is at your parents' house?"

"Oh, no, I am there, let's go," Nadeem and I pick-up the pace and follow the crowd.

It is a massive sight. I've never seen this number of people in my life before. It shakes me to my very core. It is nerve-racking. All together, all united and all asking for one thing: dignity, freedom and social justice.

"All that is necessary for evil to prevail, is for all good men to do nothing," Dr. Rashad says and laughs.

"But they didn't, they are all here, eager to shape their future. No more fear, no more humiliation," Ziko tears and laughs, picking up one of the signs.

"Ziko, where are you going?" Dr. Rashad asks.

"First, I'll return Nefertari's head to the museum; I don't need to keep it anymore. Egypt is being reborn and I have to take part in this." Ziko dissolves in the crowd.

Salma finds herself a spot. She observes; then repeats the callings in a faint voice. Dr. Rashad picks up two signs, one in each hand and goes off in a different direction yelling the callings. Nadeem's eyes are on the police officers that storm at the civilians. He cautions the protesters and guides them to move around in order to avert the brutal reaction of the police forces.

I try to look back at Salma but the crowd has swallowed her.

"You are a free man, Saad. Do what you need and want to do. Don't wait for us. Here, this is what we owe you for the ride today." Nadeem deposits some money in my hand before he too disappears.

I don't regard this as revolution, but rather a ceremony of freedom. Everyone is looking after everyone. Blocks of human beings, moving together, yelling together, chanting together, and praying together. It is amazing.

People fall injured by the police attacks. Instantly the wounded are being carried by their fellow protesters to the side. Clinics are formed in a flash. Doctors rush to the scene and medical supplies are delivered. Hospitals open their doors for free to everyone who gets shot or injured. I see foreign doctors whose destiny has dictated for them to be in Cairo today. They help the Egyptian doctors tend to the injured and the wounded in Tahrir square.

The police forces lash back aggressively. They spray the protesters with massive amounts of water. An hour later, lots of blankets are distributed among the protesters. ***"Together, we'll die together, or live together"***.

I see one of the youths been carried four times to the on-site clinics and once they fix his wounds, he is back on his feet demanding his rights as a human being. The fifth time I see him, he is blue dead with a bullet in his head. I see women, kids, seniors, disabled, religious figures, teens and youths. I see all classes and all levels of people. Egypt is on the street, in Tahrir square. I feel this is the happiest I ever felt and the proud I ever felt. I can die today and I'll be content and satisfied.

The day comes to an end but the revolution and energy of the people don't die, faint or sleep. I go and move my cab away. My cell phone is screaming in the car: "Folks are you there. So what did you decide, expedite or wait, folks?"

I head back to Tahrir square, with every step, I feel that I am a free human being who deserves to be respected and treated with dignity. I walk to Tahrir square; uncertain whether I'll ever make it back home or whether I'll ever see the team again. But I walk, pick-up a sign and demand my future. Egypt is my homeland. I am not immigrating anywhere and it is in my hands to make it a better place to live in. The Tomb opens and it won't close again.

The Beginning...